David L. 1 ......

A BOY'S WAR

Sylvia

love and Best wishes

David .

AUSTIN MACAULEY PUBLISHERS™

LONDON • CAMBRIDGE • NEW YORK • SHARJAH

A CIP catalogue record for this title is available from the British Library.

ISBN 9781787104693 (Paperback)
ISBN 9781787104709 (E-Book)

www.austinmacauley.com

First Published (2018)
Austin Macauley Publishers Ltd.
25 Canada Square
Canary Wharf
London
E14 5LQ

Acknowledgements

The following names contained in this book are real – being family members, who kindly gave permission for their names to be associated with this book:

PLAISTOW
BURTON
TURPIN
BAGWORTH

The name below is the actual kapitan of the named U-Boat within this story, who sadly died some years after the end of the Second World War.

Kapitan Nollau – U-Boat Kapitan

All other names contained within these pages are fictitious and are not intend to be associated with any real persons, living or deceased.

Technical specifications on weapons and ships have been retrieved from archived material in the public domain. The events depicted are fictitious. In reality, it is true to say next to London, the city of Liverpool was the second most heavily bombed city in Britain during the German Blitz. The city was devastated and the cost of collateral damage to the civilian population was immense.

The courage of Liverpudlians during this very dark time should never be underestimated. Hope and belief in the triumph of good over evil kept the Port of Liverpool operating, remaining a vital cog in the war machine, ensuring arms and goods continued to flow to our shores from the United States of America and contributing to our eventual victory in Europe and victory in Japan. To all allied troops around the world, I would offer my most grateful thanks to survivors and those who never returned. We all owe you a debt of gratitude.

Author's Note

The characters and events in this book are fictitious; however World War II was not and sadly many millions (on both sides) lost their lives. Towns, cities, industries and institutions were destroyed, and hundreds and hundreds of years of history was lost throughout the world, pounded into the ground.

The Allies were on one side, fighting for freedom, preventing dictators from ruling the globe, defending nations less able to defend themselves. Fighting for freedom, liberty and ensuring democracy prevailed.

On the other side, the Germans, the Nazi war machine, ruled by a man, Adolf Hitler, whom history has now determined was a madman; a dictator who wanted, using that old cliché, to rule the world, intent on exterminating inferior races in a policy of ethnic cleansing. The Jewish people were one such race. He waged war for six long years throughout Europe. For some time Britain stood alone against the enemy.

Historians have written and commented on WWII in great detail and I would recommend these written works are read to understand the full horror unleashed by an uncontrollable dictator.

Whilst Hitler was the main protagonist, war also raged on other continents such as Africa and Asia, and the atrocities occurring there were no less horrific than those in Europe.

Many of those responsible for these horrors never faced justice, to answer for their crimes, they just disappeared. Hitler himself, realising the war would certainly end in defeat, took his own life, denying the world any form of justice.

Many people of my generation will still admit to there being a mistrust and animosity towards Germans in general; younger generations will have a slightly different viewpoint.

It is with thanks to William Lester Donaghy, my father, for providing an insight into the life of a young boy growing up in this troubled time. My dad was one such boy who was not evacuated, remaining in the Dingle, Liverpool, whilst the bombs fell, living with his widowed mother, my gran, Janet Donaghy.

Those memories remained with my dad until his death in 2014; he remembered them as if only yesterday. It is with great love and thanks that I unreservedly give my appreciation to him for being my dad, for surviving the tough upbringing he had and most of all, for being there for me throughout my life.

Thanks are also provided to Birkenhead Port and the 'U Boat Story' for providing technical information on U534, which was salvaged in 1993, restored and put on display in 2009 in Birkenhead, Wirral, Merseyside. The true story of this boat was the basis for the fictional U-boat depicted in this story. Acknowledgement is also given to the vessel commander, Kapitan Herbert Nollau, who survived the war and took his own life in 1968.

Thanks are also given to my family; without them, their love and support this project may never have been completed, with a special dedication to my grandchildren, Holly Grace and Samuel. May they never have to endure such events.

The bravery of our armed forces should never be underestimated, and the courage of those who went before should never be forgotten.

GOD BLESS MY DAD AND OTHERS LIKE HIM.

Technical Notes

Most of the technical information quoted in this story relating to places and equipment is technically accurate. However, for the puritans who may read this, some information and detail has been modified or changed, only for the purpose of the story.

To those I offer my unreserved apology.

No disrespect of people or events was intended.

Introduction

In Liverpool in late 1930s, although a thriving import location in the north of England, due mainly to the sea port, areas such as the Dingle were still deprived, lacking basic facilities such houses with their own lavatories. Most houses in the area shared a communal block of outside toilets.

During this time, many homes in the Dingle were 'back to back' terraced dwellings, with a lavatory section between the two rows, containing possibly four toilets. These may serve as many as ten houses.

Access to these was gained via the rear cobbled alleyways, known as entries, from the house back yard.

This was also a play area for many children of the day. Public health was in its infancy, privacy and Health and Safety were not even a glimmer in the eye.

Iron tram rails crisscrossed the streets, horse-drawn carts pounded the cobbles, competing with the odd motorcar, but mainly trams. People used bicycles or foot power. Young boys pushing wheelbarrows filled with food produce, coal, scrap or even household furniture.

Carts with metal wheel rims rattled along, horses' hooves clip clopped on the cobbles, and internal combustion engines frequently backfired from the occasional motorcar. Everywhere was noisy, the general hustle and bustle or street traders selling their wares.

Through all this, Liverpool was still an exciting place to be – there was poverty, poor housing, very few jobs apart from the docks, it had a vibrant atmosphere. Because of the importance of the river and the city's trade links with the rest of the world, the noise to be found there was of different voices – Irish, American, West Indian, Jamaican, Indian and Chinese. In fact Liverpool had a massive Chinese community, developing its own China Town.

Communities were diverse, however, it usually followed that the immigrants were employed for menial tasks only, servants to the rich living in Kensington district or St John's Place. Others were employed in restaurants or ale houses washing pots, cleaning floors and the like.

But the city was alive, the docks were one of the busiest in Britain, sailing ships of all sizes entering the port, it would be true to say that many sailors jumped ship in Liverpool in search of better things.

The city of Liverpool was famous for the ferry crossings to Birkenhead, Wallasey and Woodside. One of the first known ferries to cross the river was in 1814. In those days it was a sail boat, not much bigger than a rowing boat, but it was able to transfer about a dozen people and some supplies.

Manned by a single ferryman, in poor weather, the crossing would have been hazardous, but to make the journey by coach and horse would have taken three or four times as long, travelling into Cheshire and then along the coast line, passing Ellesmere Port and Elton and further still to Woodside.

The River Mersey was in those days the same as modern day motorways; vessels of all sizes navigating the waterway, the hustle and bustle of a major seafaring city.

Things between 1940 and 1942 took a turn for the worse. Although the Second World War commenced in 1939, it was 1940-42 which totally changed the face of Liverpool. Outside London, Liverpool was the second most bombed city in the United Kingdom.

The German Luftwaffe carried out a sustained bombing campaign against the city. That is stated with no intention of undermining the dreadful hardship other cities also endured, but Liverpool had the unique distinction of being the main route from America in receiving supplies to support the war effort.

This served only to further the suffering endured by the people of Liverpool. The winter of 1940 was in particular very hard, already months of bombing, the infrastructure failing, shortage of food, coal and dairy products – even housing – the people were on their knees.

Chapter One

It was one of those nights when you imagine something was going to happen. There was a full moon, and the sky was clear. Black, but clear! Strangely there were few stars to be seen, and no wind to speak of. The city waterfront landscape, recognised around the world, silhouetted against the light reflection from the River Mersey, rose majestically skywards.

The air was still and very few lights to be seen. In fact the only lights on show were those coming from the entrance to the tiny, but quaint, Dingle railway station, located just outside Liverpool city, in the Toxteth district, Liverpool 8.

Although the station was actually underground, the street level entrance was illuminated. A single bulb gave a dim glow, expanding only a few feet from the entrance. In fact during these war years, communities were very cautious regarding lights – there were stiff penalties for those discovered showing lights during the blackout.

It had been snowing, but stopped now, the snow seemed to glisten in the light. It was cold, very cold. The scene resembled a typical Christmas card drawing. But in Liverpool in 1940, no-one would really be celebrating Christmas.

The old railway station had been standing since 1893, and it didn't look as though it had changed much over that time. It was the southernmost point of the railway, near to Park Road. Even in a time of war and devastation, in the snow it looked picture perfect.

The station master, Mr Potter, would be making his final preparations of the night, waiting for the last train to arrive; it was the turning point of the rail system supporting the docks.

Southbound trains would clear the station, into the shed area, then be reversed back to the northbound line, ready to journey towards Seaforth Sands. The last train of the day was always a stay-over train.

The station was a vital link in the war effort chain. Troops, munitions, food, clothing; everything brought in by sea to help the British people, and indeed the British government, usually used tracks along this waterfront line.

From the Dingle, supplies would be unloaded and transported by other means to local and national locations.

Much of the inbound supplies came from the United States of America, who had not yet joined the war in Europe. In the not too distant future that would change; however that is another story.

Mr Potter would have the signals in place, letting the engine driver know he was clear to shunt down to the sheds. Due to the majority of the line being elevated, the track had been electrified and for obvious reasons was unsuitable for steam trains.

He had seen the weather at ground level, and was thankful that the majority of the line he was responsible for was underground, well at least the station section anyway. Once clear of the station the elevated section had no shelter from the weather. He was so looking forward to getting inside out of the cold and having a lovely hot cup of tea, if the rations permitted.

"Rations!" he muttered to himself. He was, of course, well aware that war brought difficulties, to say the least, aside from the poor lads fighting at the front, a fact he understood very well, being an old soldier from the Great War 1914-1918.

Tonight, and the next few nights, would prove to be far from normal. Mr Potter would talk about these nights for many years to come.

Meanwhile, tucked up next to a small but warm open coal fire at 10, Mill Street, Freddie Bloom sat watching the flames flicker and dance in the grate. Small embers flicked from the coals onto the hearth. The fire guard was in place so the embers were unable to reach the carpet in front of the fire.

Freddie and his mum, Janet, spent every night in the back kitchen of their Victorian terraced house. A small valve radio crackled away in the corner. Usually it was only turned on to keep up with the news; there wasn't that much on anyway. But announcements were made and people needed to know.

No television these days.

At the outbreak of war, Mrs Bloom had wanted Freddie to be evacuated with other local children, but she knew that she needed him there; after all he was working and bringing home a few pennies each week.

His mum needed this; she had been born with a slightly shorter left leg, and walked with a pronounced limp. Working was hard for her, but she went out every single day doing any menial jobs she could, which included charring for the well-to-do residents, working in the local Park Road wash house.

Freddie, a rotund little boy, born in January 1928, was often ridiculed because of his weight and earned the nickname Uncle Fester. He was small for his height to weight ratio, dark brown almost black hair, glistening blue eyes and a smile to melt hearts, usually dressed in hand-me-down clothing, or items freely given from the district mission. He was just twelve years old when war broke out.

His mother didn't know, but he even smoked cigarettes.

He earned a little money working for Albert Jones, delivering milk, quite often waking up Albert at five a.m. each morning, banging on the dairy rear doors.

Usually though he was paid in the form of sterilised milk; he drank pints and pints of it each day whilst helping Albert. This may have been the reason he gained his weight. He would sit on the horse-drawn milk float, helping himself to the displayed bottles.

Tonight his mum toasted a slice of bread on the open fire; due to the lack of any real intense flames, it usually took a while. She used an old metal fork which to Freddie looked like the Devil's fork.

A saucer with a chunk of butter lay in the hearth, slowly melting from the warmth of the fire. Mum would leave it there

14

just long enough to be soft for spreading on the toast, but not too long that it would be like water. She seemed to know just the right time.

Due to rationing, it was only a small chunk, and only one thinly cut slice of bread between them. Before the war, times were hard anyway for the poor people, but these days, a mouse wouldn't survive on their portions.

Dressed in his cowboy and Indian patterned pyjamas and dressing gown, which had been a hand-me-down from a neighbour, Freddie always looked forward to this before he went to bed.

The faint glare from the fire made the back kitchen look like a sunset, if only a small one, red and yellow flickers bouncing off the walls and the ceiling. It felt so cosy, if not that warm. The flickering would have lit up the cobbled back yard, if the blackout curtains had not been drawn.

The local ARP wardens patrolled every night; it was an offence, under wartime law, to expose a light during the blackout, even cars and buses had to travel in the dark. Horse-drawn carriages were not allowed to display any carriage lights either.

"Have you fed the chickens?" Mum said.

"Yeah! I did it before, Mum," Freddie answered, in his thick Liverpudlian accent.

"Good boy," his mother would answer.

Janet Bloom knew what it was like to have a hard upbringing, having been sent to the local Toxteth workhouse aged only three years old. Although she never really knew it, in later life she suspected it was due to her deformity.

The workhouses were buildings set aside for the homeless, the neglected and the few who were not born 'quite right'. Many children were sent there just because their mother, usually unmarried, couldn't afford to keep and support them.

Janet was one such child. Born in 1904, sent to the workhouse in 1907, she had remained there until she was eighteen. Sharing a dormitory with up to twenty other children, she had slept in a single iron bed, under springing supported a thin mattress. If lucky, two blankets.

The children sent to the workhouses were often treated like second class or even third class beings. No home comforts, the bare minimum needed to survive and work. In winter the dormitories were freezing cold, a small single hearth at one end housed a barely lit coal fire – ice usually formed on the inside of the windows.

Whilst there, she had to earn her way, working very long hours cleaning, working on her hands and knees scrubbing the wooden floors, washing bedding – in fact, like all the children there, she was used as slave labour.

But she was fed and watered every day. But it was a tough introduction to the world, aged three years old.

She remained there for years, only leaving aged eighteen. It would be fair to say she had become institutionalised. Told what to do and when to do it!

In the short period before she finally left, she actually earned a few shillings for her work. This was designed to help her pay her way in the bigger world, when she would have to stand on her own.

She married her husband, William, in 1919. A veteran of the 14-18 conflict, the Great War, he was a soldier with the Irish Fusiliers. She had borne two children; sadly one died several days after birth. Freddie was born in 1928 and became the love of her life, more so following the death of William in 1934.

Freddie's brother was buried in an unmarked grave, a pauper's grave in the Anglican Church graveyard, near to St John's Place, Toxteth

It would be a regret for Freddie in later years that he never knew his older brother.

Times were hard for residents in the Dingle; her husband survived the Great War, only to pass over in his sleep in 1934. Cut backs and economies were a way of life for them both, everyone had to do their bit for the war effort. Due to rationing, food was scarce and queues were long.

Ration cards were issued to everyone – without one and an ID card, you couldn't obtain food at all.

One way to make the rations go further was to acquire chickens; at least they would have fresh eggs and occasionally meat. Many urban households raised poultry in back yards, sheds, anywhere they could. It helped on a daily basis; rations were what they were – rations! Barely enough to survive on, eggs, often powered eggs, and meats, were very hard to come by, communities often queuing for hours only to find by the time they reached the front, the supply had run out.

Queuing became a fact of life during this period.

"I made sure they were tucked in nice and warm too, Mum," said Freddie.

"That's my boy," Mum smiled her reply.

Freddie was only twelve years old, but recent times had been very hard for him and his mum. The only work she could obtain was working long hours in the local wash house, which was hot and tiring work, fishing clothing from huge industrial washers, lugging them over to a massive drier, and all this for a shilling a week. (Today a shilling is just five pence.) Not wanting her son, Freddie, to be evacuated, he was supposed to still attend school, but most days the school closed due to the overnight bombing from the Luftwaffe – Liverpool was pounded night after night, much the same as London, and other major ports and cities, with them being major links and routes for supplies and arms.

Freddie didn't mind too much as he hated school. Also, he wasn't what would be termed as academic; most of his friends were still away in the countryside with evacuation families. He was one of a very few 'almost' teenagers remaining at home. Apart from babes in arms most of the children had been sent away for safety reasons. Older children were allowed to stay, if their parents could evidence that they were needed in the home environment.

The English countryside was hardly ever bombed; except for those areas containing RAF airfields, the Germans wouldn't waste bombs on sparsely populated farming areas, unless their planes were in trouble and had not completed their target run. They would drop their loads to make it easier to return to their home base.

Life in the country was totally different to that in the towns and cities. The only indication that the country was at war was the land army of female workers. Town women moved to work in the fields under the campaign 'Dig for victory'.

The idea was that with the menfolk fighting, the women took over jobs on farms, and for that matter in the factories. They were used in munitions factories. They were used in aircraft hangers, building bombers and fighters for use by the RAF.

There was no pressure on the women, but it was frowned upon if they refused to go and stayed at home. However, many did, but they busied themselves in other ways of assisting the war effort.

Renovating clothing, making new from old, if they were a skilled seamstress or tailor their talents were harnessed.

The heavy snow over the last few days had caused drifts, some ten feet in places, bringing the Dingle to a virtual standstill. The people who were lucky enough to have a motorcar or motorcycle found petrol was rationed; as a result, transport was considered a luxury, the common denominator was that people walked. The blackout also made travel difficult; vehicles had to have light hoods fitted, giving the smallest little slit of light to see ahead. In the pitch black of night, seeing people or objects in the street was more or less impossible.

But Freddie didn't mind the cold and the snow.

Freddie had been spending lots of time at Dingle railway station, he loved trains and he got on well with old Mr Potter. In fact he would help the station master most days of the week with minor tasks and chores at the station, after he had finished his milk round with Albert Jones.

"Time for bed, my darling son," said his mother.

Freddie kissed her goodnight and made his way out from the back kitchen to the hallway, which was freezing cold.

Freddie and his mum lived in an old council-owned terraced house on Mill Street; from the front door they had a clear view straight down to the river. It was an old Victorian house, which may have been occupied in days past by rich people or landowners. The hallway was a hundred feet long, with a grand staircase halfway down, leading to the first floor and its four bedrooms. To one side of the staircase was the cellar entrance door. This area was almost as large as the upstairs.

It was impossible to heat the whole house. His mum only had limited amounts of coal; usually it was what Freddie could find in the street after the coal man had passed by, two or three lumps at a time. Coal was in very short supply, so the other open fires in the house were very rarely lit. It was mainly the one in the back kitchen.

Sometimes when he was out on his milk round, Freddie would collect any lumps of coal he saw in the street. He had learned it paid to keep his eyes on the ground, all sorts could be found. Sometimes even a penny had been found – *finders keepers,* Freddie thought.

Like food and everything else, coal was rationed; after all, the coal miners were all working towards the war effort. Some people not called up to fight, a high proportion being children, under Mr Bevan were conscripted to the mines and later became known as the Bevan Boys. Miners were classed as being in a reserved occupation.

This was hard work and Freddie was expecting to be sent down the mines very soon. Many children worked within the coal pits; according to the council lists, Freddie Bloom had been evacuated, so as yet he hadn't been called to enter the pits.

Racing along the lobby, which is what Liverpudlians called the hallway, and up the stairs, Freddie arrived at his bedroom

19

at the front of the house, grabbed the blankets from the bed whilst he watched the night sky from his window.

Wrapped in his blanket he watched.

No lights inside and blackout curtains in place of course.

The sirens had already sounded, the bombs would soon be coming again and due to the enforced blackout no street lights were lit and only the tiniest of lights could be seen from the railway station entrance.

Mr Potter will be for it now! Freddie thought.

The air raid wardens were most forceful in their adherence to the blackout. Under no circumstances should the residents provide a guiding light to the Nazi bombers.

It was thought that British survival depended on it.

"Put that light out!" This sentence was commonplace, probably in every British town and city. The ARP wardens patrolled the town; it was vital that no lights shone; as the Dingle was located so close to the docks, it would be like an open invitation to the enemy bombers, showing them the way to the ships and vital supply storage areas.

"Put that light out!" These words were heard nightly.

Meanwhile, far out in the blackness of the River Mersey, unbeknown to the town residents, a sinister development was taking place at sea, way out in the blackness.

Freddie then saw the small chink of light go out at the railway station; he continued watching for a short time and it stayed out. The only other thing happening was a couple of soldiers home on leave, walking under the overhead railway – known locally as the 'Dockers' Umbrella'.

The actual railway opened in 1893. It ran from Dingle to Seaforth Sands, cutting straight along the waterfront, passing the Liver Building, Kings & Queens Docks, the Albert Dock and eventually onward to Southport, Lancashire.

At least the soldiers would be out of the snow, which had started to fall again.

Freddie listened to the sound of hobnail boots against the paving and cobbles, echoing in the quiet night. He mimicked the soldiers and marched across his bedroom floor. He would join up as soon as he could, providing the war lasted that long. It was a common thought that everyone had to do their bit.

In the distance, Freddie heard that all too familiar sound, the drone and then the whine as the bombs fell. Searchlights lit up the sky, the anti-aircraft batteries searched for the invaders and bringers of doom. He hated the Third Reich and the Luftwaffe and all they stood for, and the fact they were here night after night, destroying homes and killing innocent people, made his hatred even more intense.

What Freddie didn't know was when the bombing would cease, once and for all.

Some of the homes on Mill Street had metal half rounded shelters, sunk into the rear gardens; if they didn't have a garden, they were bolted to the ground in the back yards. Local allotments had an abundance of shelters; these were known as Anderson shelters.

But to be honest many people didn't use them, they preferred to sleep in the comfort of their own beds. But that was risky, certainly in these early days of the war. After the first few raids, people seemed to become complacent; 'it won't happen to us' attitude.

Freddie's room was lit from the searchlight based on the rooftop at Wellington Road School, just a hundred yards from his house. The sounds were getting louder now, the droning and the whining and then the explosions, one, then another, then another, until it was impossible to distinguish the individual explosions. It just seemed like a continuous explosion. Fire brigade bells echoed through the streets.

Rat-tat-tat-tat! The ack guns burst into life. Through the window, Freddie saw aircraft silhouetted in the searchlights. It seemed the AA guns were blasting away from all directions.

Their success rate wasn't great, but sometimes they brought a plane down, which always lifted the community's spirits, with residents chatting about it for days. These successes were broadcast in newspapers and on the wireless. Just bringing one enemy plane down gave Scousers a sense of pride.

"Freddie! Freddie! Quickly now!" his mother shouted. The panic in her voice was clear. Instead of going outside, his mother always took him down to the cellar; she had put an old bed in there with blankets and pillows; for some reason she always felt safer there than outside.

Bounding down the stairs, Freddie met his mother at the bottom and they both hurried down into the cellar. It was safer than staying upstairs, but it didn't offer too much protection. If there was a direct hit on the house Mrs Bloom knew they would likely be buried alive, if they survived the initial blast. But they felt safer anyway. Buried under countless tons of rubble, their chance of actually surviving would be poor to say the least.

The explosions were right on top of them now, the noise was terrifying. The planes must be coming right up the street; that's how it seemed to Freddie anyway. The street level windows in the cellar were blown out in an instant. One after another, the bombs crashed down; after the noise, there was the searing heat – incendiaries, designed to cause as much damage and destruction as possible.

The Germans seemed intent now to bomb the spirit out of the people, which they clearly thought would affect the government – pound the public into submission!

The house next door was gone! The shock wave from the explosion caved in the ground level of number ten. Freddie and his mum were tossed across the floor like balsa wood. They were sent crashing into the far wall.

Glass fell like snow.

The searing heat from the blast was in total contrast to the freezing night air, which was now sweeping right through the cellar. Although Freddie was not aware, the noise and confusion outside was unbelievable.

Mrs Bloom knew the upstairs had gone, she heard the roof collapsing, rubble and masonry crashing to the ground above their heads. She thought it may not have been a good idea to stay in the cellar after all.

The noise was horrific, a wall of sound, explosions, buildings being ripped apart by high explosive incendiaries, screams and shouting, crying and moaning, bells clattering everywhere. Urgent voices shouting, "Is there anyone in there?" It seemed like the whole street had been blasted to bits.

How the people suffered. Looking back in later life, Freddie would proclaim this as totally barbaric. But this was the era he was growing up.

The freezing night air burst into the cellar, together with the smell of burning, bricks, flagstones, cobbles and anything else the bombs had torn and shattered from their normal resting place.

Fires raged in the street. There were giant craters in the road, some twenty feet or more deep.

Fire hoses zigzagged across the road, men running in all directions, shouting orders, screaming for more water. The sound of bombs falling and exploding was now replaced by the sound of buildings falling. Flames ripped high into the sky. Black smoke, this was a vivid memory for Freddie.

Sometimes the Nazi war machine targeted the docks, other times the bomber crews were just dumping their loads if their aircraft had been hit, or if the weather was bad and they couldn't see a target. It was easier for them to drop them anywhere and get away from the ground guns.

It seemed like it was just for the heck of it! That's how it appeared to Freddie.

As quickly as they had arrived, the Luftwaffe left. However the noise didn't stop there. Fire bells still rang out, voices shouted, people searching houses looking for survivors, sometimes whilst the fires still raged. Firemen pumped water as quickly as they could, but usually it was a waste of time; incendiaries set fire after fire. Local people were out with stirrup pumps, which were totally ineffective with the scale of the fires.

The night sky glowed red! Firemen, ambulance men and communities came together to try and control the carnage.

Freddie knew these fires would rage on for hours, long after the filthy Hun had returned home, to their children.

Tonight they were lucky; whilst the front of the house had been blown out, there was fresh air coming, which indicated a gap to escape. As Freddie and his mum emerged through the massive gap in the cellar, bleeding and dazed, the scene was one of panic. Buildings burnt, collapsing even whilst the firemen were fighting the fires. Mill Street had been blown apart! The road was no longer what you would call a road, it resembled the surface of the moon with potholes everywhere, bombed out houses. Bessemer Street, Beloe Street, Harlow Street right down to Dingle Mount – all gone.

Wellington Road School was no more!

Freddie wondered if the chink of light at the railway station had guided the filthy Hun to Mill Street.

He also wondered if old Mr Potter was okay, as the docks had taken the brunt of the attack – as usual.

"Watch out, lady!" a voice shouted, and the owner of that voice was pointing to a house two doors away. The front wall was collapsing; rubble tumbled to the ground, sending plumes of smoke rising into the air.

There was a smell in the air.

Freddie and his mum dived to the ground, desperately praying that the falling brickwork would miss them. Miss them it did, more by good luck than anything else. Lying on the cold ground, covered in snow and dust and rubble, they lay not moving and silent. The noise of the scene seemed to fade. They couldn't hear a thing, apart from ringing in their ears.

After what seemed an eternity, although in fact it was only a few minutes at most, rushing onlookers dashed to their aid. The ARP warden was there helping Freddie's mother to her feet. Her concern was with Freddie.

Firemen desperately tried to extinguish fires, ambulance men covered the dead and walked away, bodies everywhere. People who survived were sitting amongst the rubble, on the snow-covered ground, seemingly unaware of the cold, bruised and battered, bleeding, crying.

"My son! Where is he? Is he all right?"

"He's here, my girl," said the warden, smiling to try and reassure her.

In the carnage, she saw Freddie sat in the rubble, a fireman cleaning around his mouth, making sure he could breathe properly. Freddie was covered head to foot in dust, with a streak of red coming down his face. This was blood, a deep head wound. Freddie was dazed and confused, but his injury had not been caused by the collapsing wall, but from the initial bomb impact during the raid.

Shards of glass splattered his face.

An ambulance man was tending to Freddie now, cleaning a wound to the side of his head.

"Oh my word!" Freddie's mum was sobbing out of control. "Your head!" She took hold of him and squeezed him so tightly; Freddie had to try to push her away to breathe.

She licked the corner of her blouse and wiped the dust from his face.

"I'm okay, Mum," he said.

Wrapping a bandage all the way round his head, the ambulance man helped Freddie to his vehicle, an old Ford 8 being used as a makeshift ambulance, which was originally black, but now due to the war it was painted white with a large red cross on the sides and roof.

"I can't spare more than this!" said the attendant. He then left to tend to others.

He handed Freddie's mum a single spare bandage. Medical supplies, like everything else, were in short supply.

"Change the bandage in a day or two, go and see your own doctor too. That's if you can find him in this bloody mess!"

"Thanks you so much," smiled Freddie's mum.

"Now love, take him to the mission for a cup of tea. They won't let you back into the house until it has been checked and passed safe, but looking at the state of it, doubt you'll get back in there, it looks like it's too far gone. You need a brew too, I think, " said the medic.

The old Sailors Mission was just along Mill Street, which by pure chance hadn't sustained any damage, certainly none that was noticeable. The front windows had long ago been boarded up against blast damage; it had been used to offer shelter since the beginning of the war, one of the focal points when the war came to Liverpool.

Traditionally the Mission, as the name suggested, was a sleeping place for sailors, a bed and hot meal for any seafarer arriving in the port. Like all the buildings, it was Victorian and of substantial size, a landmark for years. The front door was church-like, arched top with a semicircle of glass panels. The stained glass panels depicted ocean scenes.

Artillery stations had fallen silent now, it may be sometime before any news filtered out showing any success they may have had. If they hit anything, wreckage would be recovered sooner or later. It always heightened spirits when news came through of a kill! And a kill meant that an enemy plane had been shot down or damaged enough to cause it to crash and burn.

Several fewer Nazis to fight.

Freddie thought back to the night before, when he had seen the rooftop searchlights burst into life as the raid began – now it was gone! How many men lost their lives there last night?

Wellington Road School was famous for its rooftop playground, the only school in Liverpool to have one – most unusual in its design – but gone now, nothing but rubble and a hole in the ground. He and many of his friends had attended the school before the war.

In these desperate times, any such news was a boost to the British people and at the moment, the people needed a boost. This small nation stood alone against the mighty German war machine crushing everything in its path. Poland could testify to that.

Freddie and his mum joined dozens of other local families being cared for inside the mission building. There were also people from neighbouring districts taking comfort there; it was a case of any safe place in a storm. That night the storm would very probably come again in the guise of the Luftwaffe.

Ladies handed out blankets or whatever they had to hand, a small biscuit and a mug of tea. If lucky, you could get a sprinkling of sugar, but only if you were lucky.

These were stern-looking ladies, some spoke in Scottish, some in Irish, there were even some black ladies there, immigrants from the Commonwealth and indeed the rest of the world, who arrived in Liverpool by sea, searching for a better life. A better life! Not on this day anyway; this day could not be described as better.

Meanwhile, at Dingle railway station, Mr Potter surveyed his section of line, rubble and the remnants of destroyed buildings and trees strewn across the track. The station itself had escaped any real damage. The waiting room was still intact. The ticket office was still in one piece and the left luggage room was undamaged.

"Thank heavens for small mercies!" he said. He treasured his beloved railway, having been involved with engines, tracks and stations all his working life.

The track still needed to be cleared as troop trains rolled through on a weekly basis, transferring soldiers from the docks to barracks around the country. Many would be London bound eventually, to join the battle groups to cross the Channel, whenever that would be. But Winston Churchill told the people on a daily basis that we would go to the aid of France and fight the Nazi machine.

'Europe must not fall.'

As Mr Potter moved along his track, the local Volunteer Force, or Home Guard as they became known, arrived at the station. They had been deployed there by the local regular military commander, to assist with the clean-up, as the importance of this line could not be overestimated.

Well at least the snow has stopped! he thought. But the weather was the least of his worries.

"Morning, Potter," barked Captain Siddlington-Brown.

His Home Guard unit was made of older Liverpudlians, too old to join up and sign on to fight, but people who wanted to do their bit for the war effort. That was the spirit found wherever you went throughout Britain at this time.

Some locals ridiculed them as toy soldiers, but each and every one of them was proud to serve; if accepted every one of them, to a man, would have gone to fight. Some were veterans from WWI, The Great War. Historians and politicians called it 'the war to end all wars', but there was nothing great about it. Yet again it was senseless killing. The war to end all wars; how wrong could they have been.

There were some in the volunteer force though that had avoided the call-up, due to medical conditions. Some were just too old! Some were in reserved occupations.

"Morning, Captain. We copped a load again last night," said Mr Potter.

"Indeed Potter, those filthy cowardly Hun bombing innocent people. Well, our good, brave boys will be giving it to them tonight I shouldn't wonder," answered Siddlington-Brown.

"Blow them to bits, I'm hoping," said Potter.

"Quite!" Blowing them to bits was not playing the game in his mind. His public school education dictated that war was like a gentleman's game – soldiers removed but in a nice way! Life wasn't at all like that in reality.

Back at the mission, Freddie Bloom and his mother sipped hot tea with sugar, and had been wrapped in blankets for warmth. This was the age-old remedy for shock; did it work? Well, people did it anyway. The mission ladies were nice, they cared about people.

"How are you my dear?" said Father Fitzgibbon, the Dingle parish priest. He was an interfering man, but a man of God, who obviously prayed every night to keep his flock safe.

"Not too bad, Father," said Mrs Bloom.

"And this little fellow?"

"He was hurt, but we are both very lucky to be alive," she answered.

"It is the power of prayer, my child."

"It's the power of a cellar, I think!" said Mrs Bloom. She was not a regular churchgoer and she thought God must be very cruel to allow this to happen every night.

"Now, my child! We mustn't allow negative thoughts to prevail!"

"All this pain and suffering! Where is God when you want him? Answer me that?" she said.

"I understand your frustration, but God is with you all the time."

"Oh go away, Father! Look at my son! Where was your God last night, eh? Eh?" She helped Freddie to his feet and stormed out of the mission.

She had an intense dislike of Father Fitzgibbon; he visited local homes, using up their rations, because it was expected to feed and water the local clergy each time they entered your house – respect they called it! Well, Janet Bloom had no respect, this was one priest who never went hungry, never went thirsty and always had a roof over his head.

Where was God when my son died and she placed him in the ground at several days old?

She had asked questions of the priest then. He couldn't answer her.

Standing in the street, she and Freddie looked at their home. A couple of walls still standing, the front was no more; wallpaper still visible in what was left of the two front bedrooms. Remains of furniture splattered in the rubble and, to make matters worse, the snow was now blowing into the shell which was once a home.

ARP wardens roamed the street, explaining which houses were safe and which were not. One said to Mrs Bloom, "Sorry, Missus, you won't be going back in there. If it doesn't come down on its own, it will have to be encouraged to."

The priest followed her outside and overheard the conversation.

"God will provide, my child," he said.

"Don't you dare, Father! Just don't you dare!" Her voice was filled with rage and the last thing she wanted was a sanctimonious priest preaching faith to her.

Mrs Bloom and Freddie were escorted away by a warden, saying, "I am told the Institute is taking the homeless today; you may like to try there." She thanked him and they slowly walked away along what was left of Mill Street, which didn't really resemble a street anymore.

There wasn't much standing apart from the Mission. Crowds wandered the area, dazed and confused, mothers with babes in arms, old age pensioners, some no doubt were veterans of the last war, hobbling along on walking sticks, mumbling words meant for no-one in particular – just words.

"Honestly, that Father Fitzgibbon! He offers only hollow words, yet he comes round knocking on doors for a donation, donations people can't afford, but they still give! What gives him the right to talk to me like that?" She looked at Freddie, shaking in her anger.

"If Dad had been here, he wouldn't have said that!" Freddie spoke softly to reassure his mum.

Freddie didn't really know his father; he had passed away when Freddie was only six years old. But he could recall how his mother spoke of him. He knew his dad wouldn't have stood for it. Just at the mere thought of his father, Freddie could feel his eyes starting to fill up.

"I know, my dear!" she replied, giving him a hug. "He did love you very much."

Even without the all clear declaration from the police and ARP wardens, soup carts suddenly appeared on the street, pushed along by some very old looking ladies. Fires were still burning, but that didn't put them off. This was what community spirit was all about. Queues started to form, as any free hand-outs were welcome.

The people looked devastated.

"Can I go to the station, Mum? To see old Mr Potter? I want to make sure he is okay," Freddie asked.

"Only if you feel strong enough, you had quite a night, you know?"

"I'm fine! Just want to see if I can help him."

"You're a good boy, Freddie Bloom. Your father would be proud of you," she answered.

"Oh go on then, but don't get in the way and be careful." She kissed the top of his head and he trotted off down Mill Street, following the Dockers' Umbrella, the overhead railway, until he reached Dingle station.

"I'll be at the Institute, see if they have any room," Mrs Bloom shouted after him, but her words were lost in the chilled air.

Heat from the fires was intense, melting the fallen snow in an instant, as he rushed along. When he reached the station, Mr Potter was seated on one of the long bench seats on the tiny platform. Mrs Potter always tried to keep the station looking pretty with colourful bedding plants, hanging baskets, anything to make it look different to what it was. It was, of course, a working railway station.

"Hello, young feller-me-lad. Glad to see you made it."

"Hello, Mr Potter. Our house was bombed last night," Freddie said.

"Yeah, I heard Mill Street caught a packet. You and your mum, okay?" asked Mr Potter.

"Yeah, not bad."

"Come here, let me look at you! Your head?"

"It's only a cut. The cellar blew in," said Freddie.

"What about your old mum?"

"She's fine too."

"Well, I am glad to hear it." Mr Potter smiled. "The cellar blew in, you say? Why weren't you both in the shelter?"

"Mum feels safe in the cellar. We have a mattress and all sorts down there."

Taking in the scene, Freddie wondered where Mrs Potter was.

"What happened here then?" Freddie asked.

"Damned Jerries! It's not too bad, will have it cleared soon with the help of the Home Guard. How's your house?"

"Not much left of it, can't go back. They say it will fall down, the ARPs say we can't stay there anymore."

"Where you going to go?" asked Mr Potter.

"Not sure, really. My mum is checking at the Institute."

"Well, young man, you tell your mum that you can stay with me and Mrs Potter in the station house. Can't have you roaming the streets. And we can't have you bedding down at the Institute."

"And my mum too?" asked Freddie.

"Of course your mum too – both of you! I can't have my best helper living out of a box, can I?"

"Ah, thanks Mr Potter, she'd love it here, I know she would." He went on, "Oh, I forgot to ask, is Mrs Potter okay?"

"She's fine my lad, strong as an ox and as brave as a lion that one! But don't tell her I said that!" He winked at Freddie.

The conversation was interrupted.

"Cooo-eee!"

"Ah, just in time! A nice cup of tea," said Mr Potter, as his wife crossed the tracks from the station house and stepped up onto the platform. She carried a small tray with a cup, a teapot and a glass of lemonade.

"I saw this young man arrive with his head all bandaged. What on earth happened? Thought you might like a brew!" she said.

Before Freddie could explain, "Just the job, my dear," said Mr Potter. "They were bombed out last night."

"Oh, my Lord!" she said. "Have some lemonade, young Freddie," she said with a smile.

"We're okay, though I got a cut on the head," Freddie said.

"Oh lord, you poor thing."

"Thanks," answered Freddie.

"That's enough, Mrs Potter; we've been through all this!" Mr Potter said impatiently. "Anyway, I've told young Freddie that he can stay with us for a while, and his mum too, of course."

"Of course they can," she smiled.

"Aw that'll be great! I always wanted to sleep in the railway station."

Mrs Potter set the tray down, poured her husband a cup of tea and handed a glass of lemonade to Freddie. "There, you drink that, it's home-made and you'll love it." Then she left.

"I'll make up the spare bed." Her voice faded away as she headed to the cottage.

Meanwhile the Toxteth section of the Home Guard, under the command of Capt. Siddlington-Brown, busied themselves removing rubble and debris from the track and the station. The Captain barked out instructions to his group of aging men.

Men too old to join up; after all, most of them had done their bit in the Great War or other conflicts around the world. But they were doing their bit again, now in the Home Guard. Some of them, of course, were medically unfit to join up to fight the Hun and not old enough to have fought elsewhere, but they were desperate to help in the war effort.

The odd one was a skiver, a wide boy and a profiteer, someone wanting to avoid the call-up and to make money from wheeling and dealing. To Captain Siddlington-Brown these types were a waste of space, but he needed men, so he put up with it. He didn't like it, but at a time of shortages, he sometimes used the wheeling and dealing practices to his advantage. To him, the war effort was all consuming.

Siddlington-Brown was a six feet tall man, strong bone structure, dark wavy hair neatly parted to the left. He had an athletic build for a man in his sixties. He had a bearing about him. He had served in the justice system for over thirty years, reaching the height of district judge; a man used to having words listened to, his actions followed and decisions unchallenged.

Chapter Two

Returning from the Atlantic and a failed sea patrol, the first sea patrol since her launch in 1942, U-534 had been ordered to make for Denmark, where upon arrival secret orders would be given to her kapitan.

The boat had spent several weeks crisscrossing the North Atlantic searching for convoy vessels. The prime aim of the U-boat fleet was to locate and sink merchant ships bound for England; if she came across a battleship all the better.

If they sank a battleship of any description, that was a bonus.

This was the life of a U-boat crew, weeks of boredom and searching, sometimes tinged with minutes of sheer excitement, the excitement of the stalk and hopefully followed by the kill.

For a boat crew to be recalled to a safe port without any form of kill was somewhat of a disgrace to the complement of men, and more so for the skipper. Kapitan Nollau was certainly feeling this embarrassment.

He was ashamed, as he knew failure was not tolerated by the German High Command. This could cost him his command, and even a posting to a desk job. In that respect he was lucky to be a sailor. Failure for an air or land commanding officer was usually followed a loss of rank and status, and sudden posting to a more hazardous area of the war theatre. Later in the war this posting was known as the Russian Front.

For sea commanders they usually just lost their ship, to someone else considered to be in favour.

U-534 was the newest class of U-boat, commissioned and launched by the German Navy in mid-March 1938. Clearly

Adolf Hitler had been planning his actions well before the outbreak of war in 1939.

Hitler, of course, was a veteran himself of the so-called Great War, 1914-1918. Following that conflict he had come to eminence within the German political system.

The boat had a length of two hundred and fifty-two feet, a total height of thirty-one feet six inches, a top speed of nineteen knots and a possible total range of some twenty-five thousand, six hundred and twenty nautical miles, built for cruising the great oceans of the world. In her day she was state of the art engineering – the perfect killing machine.

The vessel commander, Kapitan Herbert Nollau, commanded a maximum complement of fifty-six souls. Many were just boys, part of the Hitler Youth, indoctrinated in the belief that the German people were supreme and would rule the world. They were aboard U-534 to be trained for duties on other boats and the hunter packs.

In normal life, he was a family man, quite short in height, which was a clear advantage working in such tight confinement. He was slim in build, but with a deceptively stern voice, which seemed out of place with his general stature.

"Attention! Attention! This is the Kapitan. We have orders to sail to Denmark. I know you are disappointed we did not engage our enemy and the chance to serve the Fatherland. We will have another opportunity and you will make the Fatherland proud, but not today." Kapitan Nollau replaced the microphone and turned off the intercom.

"Captain! Why are we being recalled?" his first officer, Klaus Hoffmann, asked.

"I cannot say, but when I know, you will know."

Unbeknown to Kapitan Nollau, U-534 would be embarking on one of the most daring raids of the war, a raid which would strike at the heart of Britain and one of the most concentrated ports outside of London.

Most of the men, equipment and supplies came to Britain through Liverpool. A port with a long history, the main trade route between Britain and America, tens of thousands of men were disembarked there, ready for onward movement throughout the homeland for training and transportation to Europe.

U-534 was more than up to the job; she was armed to the teeth, having six torpedo tubes, four positioned in the bow and two to the stern; she also had 20mm AA guns and a deck-mounted 105mm gun, firing one hundred and twenty rounds per minute.

Most frightening of all, certainly as far as the allies were concerned, she was carrying three T11 experimental torpedoes with acoustic homing systems, which were a countermeasure to the British Foxer decoy system.

This one boat could cause devastation to the British fleet.

Running silent and deep to her maximum depth of seven hundred and fifty feet, U-534, using her twin nine litre turbocharged engines powered her way towards the Danish coast; the last thing her kapitan wanted was to engage the enemy at this time. He had ordered silent running to avoid any possible contact with the British fleet, even if this meant not having a free pop at a loose or separated convoy ship.

Slowing and turning, zigzagging across convoy channels, it would take U-534 and her crew five days to reach Denmark. They would be out of contact with High Command for that time, as Kapitan Nollau would not risk rising to deploy the radio mast; avoid detection at all costs were the last orders he received.

Kapitan Nollau was to meet with the Oberkommando der Kriegsmarine (Naval High Command) and Seekriegsleitung (Naval War Staff). He was aware that Admiral Schniewind (Chief of Staff, Naval War Staff) and Vice Admiral Lutjens (Naval Commander West, C in C Fleet) would both be present.

He would have to convince them both and others that he was worthy of their trust and support. It was unlikely the Fuhrer would be there; however, his actions were unpredictable, to say the least.

It had been known by most officers, Hitler's desire to invade Britain; this had been apparent from the start of the war and even prior to that. The humiliation of the armistice had never left his thoughts; for the all-powerful German nation to surrender was the biggest insult of all.

Prior to 1939, the West had long considered Adolf Hitler to be a madman, a very dangerous man, an opinion that was now being played out. His brutal attack and swift takeover of Poland, his relentless move into France – he swept through the Maginot Line like a knife through butter.

The next stop would be Britain.

Kapitan Nollau was under no illusions that a wrong word spoken, a misguided glance – the slightest hint of disapproval would be his downfall.

It would be a time for discretion; agree even if he didn't, show positive attitude, even if doubt was at the forefront. He had to be clever, yet not too clever. His future depended on that.

The crew of U-534 were lacking the air they had shown days earlier; a young crew full of confidence and expectation. Now, without a kill to their credit, they were being recalled. The air of unease was multiplying through the boat.

The senior officers were not blind to the feelings and First Officer Klaus Hoffmann had attempted to point this out to Kapitan Nollau; this had not gone down well.

Chapter Three

"Come on chaps!" Captain Siddlington-Brown said. "Put your backs into it!"

The Home Guard captain gave the orders; he thought it would not be the done thing to actually get his own hands dirty. He simply told his men what to move, where, and when to move it. A point not missed by the Home Guard volunteers.

Sergeant Struthers, a mechanic during the day, rolled his eyes and winked at Freddie. "One of these days he'll get his shiny boots dirty."

Freddie had made his way along the track to greet the Home Guard.

"Can I help, Mr Struthers?" Freddie asked.

"Good boy, want to do your bit, eh Freddie?" Sergeant Struthers said.

"Yes, sir!"

"Sergeant! Never mind all that, carry out your orders!" interrupted Captain Siddlington-Brown.

"Sir! Sorry, Freddie." Struthers smiled and walked away, heading towards the end of the platform.

"Mr Potter, why does the captain act like that? Why can't I help?" Freddie was confused; he thought everyone should be helping in some way.

"Now then, son, don't you worry, the captain is a good man, if sometimes a little foolish, or critical of the others."

"But I want to help. I want to help get your station working again."

"I know, and believe me, you will," Mr Potter answered. "Now just enjoy your lemonade."

Freddie's mum arrived at the station and was immediately greeted by Mrs Potter. "Come dear, you sit down, my lovely."

"Thank you so much, you're so kind."

"Nonsense. We all have to do what we can."

"Thank you. I hope Freddie isn't getting in the way?"

"Not at all, my dear," Mr Potter interjected.

"Everything's in a mess at the moment, we took a couple of hits last night, but mostly it was the track, and as long as the kettle still works, we'll be fine," Mrs Potter joked.

Finishing his tea, Mr Potter rose and pointed towards the track just beyond the platform. "Come on, Freddie, come with me, I need to check the track down there. I want you to look for damage."

"Great." Freddie leapt to his feet.

"Now, Freddie, don't you get in the way!" said his mother.

"I won't, Mum, don't worry."

"He'll be fine, Mrs Bloom," Mr Potter offered.

"Sorry to hear about your house," Mrs Potter said.

"We were lucky, we got out. Others didn't, so we can't complain."

"I have agreed with Mr Potter, you and Freddie are more than welcome to stay with us, can't have you going to that Institute."

"That's very kind of you both, but we couldn't impose."

"Nonsense! Think nothing of it, my dear," Mrs Potter answered.

Passing Sergeant Struthers on the platform, Freddie smiled and pushed his shoulders back, as if marching.

"When you're finished with Mr Potter, Freddie, come and see me, I'll find a job for you." The sergeant winked at him again.

"Yes sir!" Freddie gave a mock salute, which was returned by Struthers, together with a beaming smile.

"Okay Freddie! Down onto the track, you check that side and I'll do this side. Look for the slightest damage, as any damage could cause the engine to come off the tracks and we wouldn't want that, would we?"

"No sir, Mr Potter."

"Even the smallest of cracks now, you tell me." Potter wanted to be sure.

Freddie never once removed his gaze from the tracks. This was an important job and Mr Potter trusted him to do it correctly. Squeaky wheelbarrows were pushed along the line between the tracks, the front wheels bouncing and sliding as they ran across the track ballast.

"Hello, Freddie," said Corporal Sam Burton, approaching with a barrow. "You may want to check the track about a hundred yards down; just removed this lot from it, looked like there may be a crack."

"Okay Sam… er sorry, Corporal!"

"Yes sir, Private!" Sam Burton responded with a smile. "You'll make a good little soldier one day, Freddie."

"I hope so, Corporal."

"Be careful what you wish for, Freddie. This is not a good war, stay out of it for as long as you can. You hear me!" Sam Burton replied.

"Don't say that, Freddie!" interrupted Mr Potter. "This war will kill millions, mark my words." The tone in Mr Potter's voice changed; it became hard, remote, without its usual cheery attitude.

"I'm sorry, Mr Potter, I didn't mean anything by it," said Freddie.

"I know my boy – I know! It's just that this darn war is causing so much hurt and misery, homes destroyed, families destroyed, good men, young men slaughtered and for what? Yes, I know Hitler has to be stopped at all costs! But that cost will be high – that's if we win! If we lose the war, what will the cost be then?" Mr Potter stopped. He was aware that Freddie and Corporal Burton had fallen silent.

"Don't pay any attention to me!" he added.

"I'm sorry, Mr Potter; I didn't mean anything by it."

"Freddie, the war isn't all gung ho; it's a horrific event, probably more frightening than you will ever imagine," Mr Potter said.

"Carry on, 'private'," Sam Burton responded with a wink – breaking the uneasy moment.

"Come on, Mr Potter, let's check up there! We have important work to do." Freddie took hold of Mr Potter's arm.

"Good boy."

Approximately one hundred yards from the platform Freddie spotted a displacement in the track; rubble hitting the track had forced it from the sleepers. He shouted to Mr Potter and pointed to the damaged area.

"Well spotted, young Freddie!" Crouching down and inspecting the track, Mr Potter didn't like what he was seeing. "Get back to the platform, Freddie, and bring me my tools – Mrs Potter will tell you where they are – hurry now!"

As Freddie set off, running, Mr Potter shouted, "Bring the Home Guard too!"

Freddie waved his answer and continuing running.

Minutes later, Freddie, Captain Siddlington-Brown, Sergeant Struthers, Corporal Burton and others arrived to join station master Potter.

"Captain, good job we found this; if any of our troop-carrying trains hurtled through here, it would have left the rails and God knows the result! Good boy, Freddie." Mr Potter made sure any credit went to young Freddie, which made him feel very important.

"Okay, Sergeant, let's get to it. Let's get this track replaced."

"Yes sir!" Struthers directed the Home Guard with a task to complete.

"Yes, Sergeant!"

"Yes, Sergeant!"

"Okey dokey, Sarge," said Private Billy Turpin. He was the chancer of the platoon, the one who always offered to get something or other – but at a cost! The type of soldier Captain Siddlington-Brown disliked, but had to put up with.

"That's sergeant to you, Turpin!"

"Yes, sergeant!" Turpin replied, standing to attention, with humour in his actions.

"Oh never mind, Billy – just get on with it!" Struthers said less formally. He liked Turpin, even though he knew he was a wide boy; but he also knew that if the platoon needed something, he could get it – and that benefited them. And anyway, what the Captain didn't know was sometimes for the best. (When Turpin 'acquired' anything, although it left a feeling of distaste with the Captain, he turned a blind eye and always used whatever the item was to improve the platoon.) If Siddlington-Brown ignored where it came from, it was all right!

Running back to the station, the Home Guard snapped the padlock off the stores shed, grabbed pickaxes, shovels, heavy lump hammers, pins and brackets, chisels and ballast; all were piled into wheelbarrows. Cutting gear and track lifting claws were packed into another. All were pushed at speed from the shed to beyond the platform.

"That's it, men," Captain Siddlington-Brown said.

"There's a section of new track up by the signal box, sir," Corporal Burton said. "We could use that to replace this section."

"That's the ticket, Corporal."

"Yes, sir."

"I'll help," said Freddie.

"Good lad."

"You, you and you, with me now – let's get that track." Burton pointed to members of the platoon and off they went at the double.

Mr Potter followed, but slower; he was not as young as he used to be. "That's strange!" he said, as he neared the signal box. "That door shouldn't be open!" He was too far behind the others for them to hear him. But he wasn't happy the door was insecure. He was always careful to lock all station buildings and outbuildings. More so since the outbreak of war, as everyone was told 'walls have ears'. Everyone had to be on their guard just in case the Hun deployed infiltrators.

Meanwhile, back on the platform, Mrs Potter and Mrs Bloom had started towards the station cottage, home to the station master and his wife.

"Come in, my lovely, you should be comfortable here." Mrs Potter showed her to the small but quaint guest room. It had a small window which looked towards the platform. There was a tiny bedside lamp, with a shade covered in printed flowers. The wallpaper was of a similar style, small printed flowers in shades of red and pink.

"This is lovely, Mrs Potter."

"Please, call me Dilys. Mrs Potter seems so formal, besides it's only Mr Potter that calls me Mrs Potter. Strangely it's something we have done all our married life," she replied, with a smile and warmth in her voice.

"Then again, thank you, Dilys, the room is lovely."

"We only have one spare bed, I'm afraid. I hope young Freddie won't mind sharing with you?"

"He would sleep on the platform if I let him. He is so excited about being here – he will be fine."

"That's settled, then. I'll leave you to settle in, and please don't worry, you can both stay here as long as you like."

Mrs Bloom gave Dilys a big hug. "Thank you."

"And you must call me Janet."

"I will my dear – Janet."

Outside, the voices had an air of urgency.

"Captain! Have any of your men been inside the signal box?" Mr Potter asked.

"No! Why?"

"The door is open – and it shouldn't be!"

"Sergeant! Turpin! Check the box!"

"Okay Billy, in you go!" Sergeant Struthers shouted.

"What! Why don't you go in?"

"Just get in there!"

"What if the Hun are in there?" said Turpin.

"Then you'll be a hero when you bring them out!"

"Oh yeah, never thought of that!"

"Go on then!"

"Okay, I'm going." Private Turpin edged his way towards the door, pushing gently, just enough to get his head inside. "Hello! Is anyone there?"

Sergeant Struthers gave him a nudge and pushed him fully into the doorway. Using his Home Guard training, Turpin fell to his knees and in an almost confident voice shouted, "I'm armed! Come out with your hands up!"

"What are you doing?" Struthers asked.

"If you can do any better, Sarge, you go in!" Turpin said, in a slightly less than almost confident voice.

"Ye gods – get out of the way! This is the Home Guard. I have a dozen armed men outside. Come out now with your hands up!" He then waited.

"Don't shoot – I'm coming out." A faint voice spoke from the darkness.

Billy Turpin and Sergeant Struthers jumped backwards away from the doorway, as if taken by surprise. Mr Potter stepped forward and gently levered the door open a little further.

"That sounds like a child!" he said.

After a few seconds a little girl appeared in the doorway. It was Grace Bagworth, eleven years old and looking dirty and frightened.

"Well, sweetheart, look at you! It's Grace, isn't it, from Park Road?" said Mr Potter.

"Yes," she answered.

"What are you doing in there? You look half starved. Are you hungry?" Potter asked.

"Yes."

"Come on, darling; let's see what Mrs Potter can rustle up for you." Mr Potter took her hand and turned towards the station cottage.

Clutching the station master's hand, Grace skipped her way along the platform with Mr Potter towards the cottage. To her this was a great adventure; she, like most young girls, didn't really understand the politics of war. She did, however, understand the bombs.

She had wandered off earlier whilst her mother was helping neighbours who had suffered in the raid the night before. Park Road, like Mill Street, had once again been hit by falling bombs. In the confusion of the following morning Grace had gone in search of her friend, Freddie Bloom; she wanted to make sure he was safe after the raid.

She had told her mother, but in the confusion her mother clearly didn't hear her.

Seeing Mill Street had been devastated, she knew Freddie liked the railway; with that in mind she had raced down to Dingle station. No-one was there when she arrived, or certainly she didn't see anyone. Checking inside the signal box for Freddie – this was a spot they both snuck into on occasions – the door had closed behind her and, in her panic, she had tried pushing the door, when she should have pulled it open. She thought she was locked in.

"I will check the telephone line, we will need to call the police to get a message to your mum. She will want to know you're safe," Mrs Potter said.

Mrs Potter gave the little girl two biscuits and a drink of milk. Mrs Bloom helped; she also knew that Grace's mother would be frantic about now.

"I know her mum," Mrs Bloom said. "I will get Freddie to walk her home before it gets dark."

"Poor little mite," said Mrs Potter. "She doesn't understand what's going on; with it going dark I will have a word with Captain Siddlington-Brown, see if one of his men will take her home. It would be safer for Freddie to stay here. It won't be too long before the bombers come again, I expect."

Captain Siddlington-Brown organised Private Turpin to take the child home, as he would be on duty tonight anyway, as would the whole platoon.

"Another chance for you to be a hero, Turpin!" the Captain said. "Think you can handle that, Private?"

"Yes, sir."

"And no time wasting! I want you back here for guard duty."

With that Private Turpin reassured Grace and they both set off to walk the short distance to Park Road.

As night starting falling Captain Siddlington-Brown gathered his platoon in the station waiting room for a briefing. The platoon was on duty every night. Their role was security. The Home Guard was the first line of defence – should an invasion come. The regular army had limited resources for home defence and as a result, although they scoffed at the Home Guard, the top brass relied heavily on this 'Dads' Army' fighting force.

In the early days when the Home Guard was formed, many of the men were armed only with broom handles, pitch forks and hammers, in fact anything they could find from their everyday lives. It was only later that the brass realised that they should be armed with rifles, and more importantly, in how to use them.

The uniforms were also a later addition. At first the volunteers wore their working day clothes. Overalls, suits, whatever their day job dictated.

As normal, Captain Siddlington-Brown highlighted local telephone boxes, which would be their way of communicating should the invasion come. Road blocks were set up nightly and shoreline patrols were deployed to watch for ships.

Platoon sergeants had papers showing silhouettes of German ships and aircraft for identification purposes. It wouldn't be the done thing to raise the alarm on seeing their own planes and ships.

Equipment was shared. Things like binoculars were in short supply, so whoever was selected to use them guarded them with a certain amount of jealousy – they each wanted to be the first to discover an enemy ship coming in. Good-natured arguments took place, with one private trying to grab them from another to have a turn in gazing out. It seemed to give them a sense of importance. Weapons in the early stages were no different; the platoon had one rifle between two men.

As the war went on, this improved and each platoon member was issued with their own weapon; however, bullets totalled five each, which had to be accounted for at the end of their duty.

As the regular army needed weapons first and foremost, the volunteers got the cast-offs. Weapons such as the M1917 Enfield were purchased to support the well-known Lee Enfield rifle, but these took different sized rounds and were not compatible. Later the P19 was obtained from America, which was compatible with the 303 Lee Enfield. Other armament included the Northover projector, which was a mortar, and the Vickers gun. This was a heavy machine gun carried in their vehicle for rapid deployment, but the volunteers had few vehicles for their use, so most duty nights this machine gun was left behind.

Some nights they took it, others they didn't.

Their uniforms were ill-fitting, apart from Captain Siddlington-Brown's, who had demanded a fitted uniform as befitted his rank, a point which was a constant joke amongst the platoon. Nicknames were given such as Nelson, Napoleon and Monty. But the Captain always tried to rise above this banter.

Nothing was ever actually said to his face.

The most important thing throughout the formation of the Home Guard was the support given to the volunteer force by the First Lord of the Admiralty and Prime Minister, Winston Churchill. He had called for five hundred thousand members of the public over the age of forty, to form this home defence force nationwide.

Mr Churchill was well aware that Britain was on her knees, the armed forces were undermanned; the Royal Air Force often had nothing in reserve, the Army and Royal Navy were stretched to the limit. Things were desperate.

The nightly briefing was again interrupted as the air raid sirens sounded. This current campaign of attacks against the docks had occurred night after night; it had been going on for weeks and months now. Hitler clearly wished to pound Britain into submission. He was marching through Europe at will and the War Cabinet was obviously worried that his sights were set on British shores.

"Right, men, to your posts!" Captain Siddlington-Brown dismissed the platoon.

Searchlights lit up the sky, searching for the enemy bombers. Once they illuminated an aircraft, the lights tracked the plane for as long as possible, in order that the gun batteries had a chance to shoot them down, or to at least try.

"Put that light out!"

"Put that ruddy light out!" The ARP wardens were again on patrol; the least little light could be seen from above and was a perfect guide for the Luftwaffe navigators and bomb aimers to select a target.

"Put that bloody light out!"

Like some gigantic black hole, the lights went out over Britain.

"Mrs Potter, Mrs Bloom, Freddie, come on, into the shelter!" Mr Potter ordered. Having placed the blackout screens in the windows, all four raced to the Anderson shelter at the rear of the station cottage.

After the recent bad weather and snowfall, tonight was clear, perfect for flying. Mr Potter hoped he had plunged the station into darkness in time; he still hadn't fully cleared the tracks yet from the raid the night before. The last thing Mr Potter needed was more damage.

Explosions were heard in the distance, the drone of aircraft engines high above was getting closer. "Damn Nazis!" Mr Potter cursed Hitler and the Luftwaffe.

Air raid sirens pierced the early evening air.

Closing the shelter door, Mrs Potter had already lit a couple of candles, which was fine as the Anderson was light-proofed. All four sat down and waited. No-one spoke, they just waited, hoping they would not take a direct hit and that they would see the morning. For Mrs Bloom, thoughts of her home on Mill

Street were far from her mind. She just wanted to be able to walk from the shelter with Freddie in the morning.

But tonight would be another long night.

Silently, each one of them said a prayer.

Chapter Four

Slowly slipping in from the Irish Sea, the night was perfect, a clear sky but, most importantly, no moon.

The Luftwaffe had left and the anti-aircraft guns had long since fallen silent. The River Mersey, which should have been pitch black, was illuminated by the raging fires, the shoreline clearly visible from the river; this made navigation that much easier.

The crew aboard U-534 had been ordered to be quiet and the boat rigged for silent running. Slowly she slipped closer, running at periscope depth. Kapitan Nollau crouched over the viewfinder, watching the city burn. Whilst from his perspective it was all for the greater good and ultimate victory over Britain, he thought how senseless this was; hundreds, if not thousands, of dead and injured civilians.

In his view, this was not his war. His war was fighting other soldiers and sailors, not women and children; he was not a butcher.

Watching the city burn, his thoughts were on his home and family; were they going through the same devastation when the RAF pounded German cities?

His thoughts were interrupted as his second in command said, "Kapitan, we are at the rendezvous point."

"Yes!" he snapped back, turning three hundred and sixty degrees, scanning the whole area. "Good! No boats, no searchlights – no activity!"

"Shall I order the boat to surface, sir?"

Currently U-534 only showed approximately two feet of her outline; the periscope was the only part of her above the waterline.

"Surface – slowly!" the kapitan said.

"Yes sir." The order was given and little by little U-534 rose from the dark water; very little white water was created. It was vital that no-one saw anything; that said, everyone shoreside would have other things on their minds as the fires raged out of control.

This would be the element of surprise the master plan had called for and depended upon.

Whilst berthed in Denmark, Kapitan Nollau had been briefed by the High Command on an eyes only basis, when this audacious plan had been unveiled. Not even his second in command had been informed of their mission. The only thing he knew was that an extra complement of men had embarked with them, and that many of the boat's regular crew had been ordered to triple up in the bunk area, to accommodate the extra men.

"All stop!" whispered Kapitan Nollau.

"All stop, sir," came the immediate response.

"All hands to stations."

Crew members climbed ladders to the hatches and waited. Behind them were two lines of men, dressed in black frogman suits, breathing apparatus in place, and machine guns slung over their shoulders, shrouded with plastic coverings to waterproof them.

"Go to red!" said Kapitan Nollau. This was a signal to extinguish all white light in the boat and switch on the infrared lights; less visible when the hatches were opened.

"Open hatches."

The first new members of the crew stepped out onto the deck, keeping low so as not to present any silhouette to the opposite shore with the fires as a back light. Hushed voices sounded and then, like clockwork, small rubber bundles appeared on the deck. When in the water, they would inflate, providing rubber dinghies for the frogmen.

Several frogmen slipped into the water and the boats were lowered to them, eliminating any splash.

The boats were inflated.

The rest of the men climbed down rope ladders and entered the rubber boats. This was completed in silence. Bundles were then lowered into the boats; twelve boats in all. With the deck clear, Nollau watched from the conning tower as the fleet of small boats pushed off and were rowed toward the city shoreline.

Silent rowing – no splash.

Satisfied that U-534 had been undetected, Kapitan Nollau ordered the boat to disappear. Slowly, without any fuss or haste, she vanished beneath the water, and if anyone had looked out over the water they would have seen only the darkness.

"They're away," he said over the intercom. "I will see all officers in my ready room now. Heil Hitler." He replaced the intercom.

A new course was given to the helm and U-534 slipped from the Mersey and took up a station at her maximum depth in the Irish Sea. Her orders were to wait for an Enigma coded message from the landing party.

Twenty-four highly trained paratroopers and saboteurs covered the three hundred yards, where they were dropped, to the shoreline in a matter of minutes. They came ashore just north of the Royal Liver Building at the Pier head.

This was one of the most famous waterfronts in the world, situated between the North and South Docks. At this time several miles of the waterfront was given over to dockland. Three iconic buildings still remain to this day; the Royal Liver Building construction, completed in 1911, featuring the iconic statues of twin Liver Birds, the Cunard Building completed in 1916, and the Mersey Docks & Harbour Building (which later became known as Port of Liverpool Building), completed in 1908.

It was and still is an iconic water front.

Oberleutnant Wilhelm Shriver, a first lieutenant in the German army, was in command of the landing party. He had been briefed in Berlin by Hitler himself. He had been tasked with sabotaging key installations, mining ships in port, to actually seal the port, preventing movements. But, most importantly, he was ordered to gather intelligence and information on troop movements and defence strengths.

He was a strong twenty-two year old who had joined up as soon as Hitler mobilised his forces. He had been at the front when Germany marched into and completely overpowered Poland. He proved himself a very capable soldier and quickly rose to the rank of oberleutnant, having caught the attention of his commanding officers; as a result he had been handpicked to lead this mission.

Stowing the oars, the landing party boats drifted to the quayside. Tying up, Shriver used only hand movements to give orders, and the team were well versed with this form of communication. They knew exactly what each and every man had to do.

Silently they scaled the quayside ladders, just high enough for their eyes to peer above the harbour wall and take in the complete scene.

Fires still raged following the bombers' visit, fire bells sounded out, voices shouting and the constant thud of masonry crashing to the ground as burning buildings collapsed. An overview of the scene would have shown the devastation Liverpool as a city, as a community, had endured. The Royal Liver Building had again avoided a direct hit and was standing proud, as an icon to inspire all Liverpudlians.

More hand signals informed the landing party to advance into the shadows. They hauled their packs and bundles from the rubber boats, strapped them to their backs and darted like rats to the darkness of a shadowy world. The last man from the boats, Sergeant Franz Schmidt, used his dagger to scuttle them.

Herr Hitler had ordered them not to return. Once they had passed information to U534 they were to fight and hold out for as long as they could. This was a suicide mission.

They could not risk being discovered at first light. Once this was completed in silence, Schmidt scaled the harbour wall and joined the others in the shadows. A thumps up was given to Oberleutnant Shriver.

Running feet pounded the quayside; shouting came from all directions and metal wheels thundered by on the harbour cobbles. Holding their position Shriver and the others waited. They were aware they could be there for some time as the panic continued. But it remained their first and urgent priority to find cover, somewhere to hole up before executing the next phase of the master plan. But for now it had all gone well and to plan.

"Put that ruddy fire out!"

"Look out, that wall's gonna go!"

The constant shouting was another confirmation that the Luftwaffe had done its job again. Liverpool burned, but this was war! German cities had suffered the same fate when bombed by the RAF. To the landing party, they couldn't care less. This was war!

Swiftly and silently the landing party removed their diving suits, replacing them with everyday clothing; boots, trousers, shirts and overcoats. The swimming items were placed in empty bags and put into back packs.

They remained hidden amongst the turmoil.

Meanwhile, at Dingle railway station, Mr Potter had already emerged from the Anderson shelter, hoping that his beloved track would not have sustained further damage. To his relief, it had not.

With the dawn breaking, the rising sun was shrouded in smoke, buildings still smouldering, exhausted men sitting amongst the rubble, sipping hot tea; they had been fighting fires all night.

This was not the first night like this and it probably wouldn't be the last. They all knew this, but they came out each and every night, to play out the same roles.

No more bells ringing, no more shouting voices, just the sound of shovels and picks thumping into the debris. Dead or alive, people were still buried and the volunteers would continue until all hope was gone. After all this time, it was now more of a recovery mission as opposed to a rescue mission. But Liverpudlians, like citizens from London or Coventry or any other major city, were used to this aftermath.

Standing at the little white wooden gated entrance to the station, Mr Potter watched the rescuers and fire fighters taking a well-earned break, and wondered, *How long can we cope with this?*

"Well done, lads!" he said. "Mrs Potter will be out soon with some potted meat sandwiches, you must be hungry."

"Cheers mate!" came the reply.

"Mrs Potter! Come on, my dear, there are hungry men out here!" With great sadness in his heart he hurried towards the shelter.

Freddie appeared at the shelter door, still wearing the clothes from the night before. "How is it, Mr Potter?"

"Not too good my boy! They really hit the docks again last night."

"What about the station?"

"We're okay, once we finish fixing that section of track up by the signal box we should be okay."

"I'm getting on with it now," said Freddie, and he dashed off towards the signal box.

"Wait boy! Something to eat first!"

Freddie didn't answer as he raced along the track.

The Home Guard returned to the station. They were dirty, tired and hungry; some were injured, albeit only minor injury. They had been involved throughout the night, helping put out the fires, searching bombed buildings and cordoning off dangerous and unsafe buildings. But they knew they still had a job to do at the station, the line must remain open. It was vital.

"Morning, Private!" Sergeant Struthers said to Freddie, having a joke with the young boy and giving him a mock salute.

"Good morning, Sergeant." Freddie tried to copy the salute.

"At ease, son," the sergeant said. "I see you made it through the night! Everyone else okay?"

"Yeah, they are safe."

"A word, Mr Potter!" commanded Captain Siddlington-Brown. "They hit us hard last night, everything's a mess. What of the station?"

"We got away with it," replied Mr Potter.

"We have to get the track open today. What I am about to tell you is top secret, it goes no further. You tell no-one! Is that understood?"

"Walls have ears and all that, of course," Potter said.

"A convoy from America will be arriving in Liverpool later this morning. They held up off Ireland, being told of a possible raid on the city last night. It is vital this convoy offloads its cargo. Several ships were sunk in the Atlantic – U-boat attacks – but most made it. This line must be open!" said Captain Siddlington-Brown. "There is secret equipment being brought in. This may shorten the war – I can't say more than that!"

"It will be, Captain; you have my word on that."

"That's the ticket, Potter."

What Mr Potter hadn't been told was that the cargo was men, thousands of them, tanks, field guns, support armament, medical supplies, tons and tons of them, and food provisions. Apart from the food, the cargo would be heading south. This was the first of many such convoys over the coming days.

Equipment that would be vital for the future invasion plans, codenamed D-Day.

"Hello, Corporal Turpin. Did Grace get home all right?" said Freddie, as he saw the corporal for the first time since the air raid.

"She was as right as rain," he replied. "Hope she was okay last night though. Her mother must have taken her to a shelter, I hope."

"I hope so too," Freddie said.

Captain Siddlington-Brown marched along the track, barking his orders.

"Sergeant Struthers! Time is vital. Get that track replaced at the double. I must get a message off sooner rather than later to HQ. That track *and* this station have to be operational by 15.00 hours today. No later – is that understood?"

"Yes sir!"

"Meanwhile, Sergeant, I have to attend a meeting at command, they have some new intelligence."

"Sir!"

Captain Siddlington-Brown marched from the station to where a staff car was waiting.

"Blimey, Sarge, it must be important if they sent a car for him!" joked Private Billy Turpin.

"You heard the man, Turpin – get that track laid!"

"Yes, Sarge."

Sergeant Struthers always thought of Siddlington-Brown as a little tin god, but he was the man in charge – he who must be obeyed.

The German infiltrators had found an insecure outbuilding on land owned by The Mersey Docks & Harbour. It was a stroke of luck for them, as it was right on the docks and they had been able to slip inside un-noticed. For ease of movement, they were armed with sidearms and machine guns and grenade firing rifles only. Luger pistols were the stock sidearm within the German forces. They would not confront the English at this time unless it was absolutely necessary, as this would end their mission before it had started. Their role was intelligence gathering, troop movements, defence strengths, and once given the order, sabotage!

It was only then that they would fight to the death – no surrender.

Dressed now in their civvy clothing, the Nazis studied reconnaissance photographs of the port and surrounding area which had been obtained by the Luftwaffe over recent weeks. The landing party, who all spoke fluent English, needed to blend in, be part of the crowd in everything they did or said.

The Liverpudlian accent was not important, as this was a city with a diverse community. There were of course home-grown Scousers, with that deep guttural form of speech. There were Northeast people, from Hull, Newcastle and the like; they had come down for one reason or another, but mainly to work. There was the more than average number of Irish; micks, bog dwellers and paddies, as they were referred to.

From recon photos, Dingle railway station was about to become the focal point for the invading force; troop movements through the docks and the rail system were vital. If the Nazis could demolish these movements before they even commenced, the German war machine would benefit greatly.

The Germans had previously entered British territory, currently being in firm control of the Channel Islands Jersey, Guernsey and Alderney, where they had military rule in place. They had turned the islands into fortresses, gun emplacements staring out to sea.

They are hated, of course, by the islanders and whilst some form of relatively normal life exists, there are, as in France, pockets of resistance attempting to frustrate and derail the German war machine. But the penalties for capture were severe.

This day, the Germans had a further foothold within the United Kingdom.

Chapter Five

This old Victorian railway had been a feature of the waterfront for years, a vital link for the local economy before the war, moving everything from cotton and silk, wood, steel, concrete, right through to passengers from Liverpool to the four corners of Great Britain.

Anything which arrived at Liverpool's eight hundred year old port was moved by rail.

At the time of its inception, it was a feat of engineering. It commenced at the south end of Park Road, Dingle. On the approach to the station from the north, a half-mile underground tunnel needed to be negotiated. This had been bored out of the cliff face at the Herculaneum Dock end of Park Road.

Dingle station itself was actually opened in the winter of 1896. The plans of the day had offered further extensions with more stations; however the funding stopped and as a result no further work was carried out, further inland stations were put on the back burner, never to be realised.

Its history was not without incident. In December 1901, due to an electrical fire which resulted in six deaths, the station and line were closed for a number of months.

History would show that Dingle station finally ceased operation and closed its doors on the thirtieth of December, 1956. Many thought it a sad day.

Running mainly through the dock area, the dockers' umbrella was founded on an iron structure raised above street level by some sixteen feet and running for an estimated six and a half miles.

From inception through its build, it had been designed to be electrically powered with a 'live' rail located in the centre of the track. The station originally operated with three staff; the station master, the signalman and a carriage cleaner.

During the war years many of the other stations along the docks were bombed numerous times. However, due to its importance, the line was always patched up and repaired, the trains would continue to run as soon afterwards as possible. The Dingle section suffered in the same way.

Mr Potter, a born and bred Liverpudlian, had worked on the railways all his life. He had been promoted to station master in 1933; with that came the benefit of the station cottage. He and his wife had enjoyed several good years living there prior to the outbreak of war. It was fair to say they had the idyllic lifestyle; a country style cottage on the outskirts of a major city.

How quickly things change. With the onset of war, initially it had seemed so far away, Europe was a world away from his life in Toxteth. Then the bombing started.

If he survived this horrible war, it would take years, he often thought, to get back to those days – if that was possible.

Chapter Six

Two days after the landing, Oberleutnant Wilhelm Shriver and his detachment of troops had hidden themselves well, a practice they were well versed in doing; constant training, survival exercises, self-control and, above all, that German discipline, all played a part.

Dingle railway station had been their objective. To that end the mission had already been successful, intelligence gathering and covert observations, but above all, non-detection at this stage.

"Schmidt!" whispered Oberleutnant Shriver. "Weapons!"

"Herr Oberleutnant."

Sergeant Schmidt shuffled amongst the landing party, tapping and pointing to the array of different armaments carried by the group. "Check and re-check!" With, what we later came to associate with the German race, precision and intense concentration, each member of the team pulled back the hammer, clicked it closed, loading a round into the weapon breech. If nothing, they were prepared.

Freddie Bloom had awoken early that morning; the horror of the previous night was forgotten for a short time. Dingle railway station had yet again survived. He leapt from the bed, leaving his mother to sleep; he ran outside and greeted a new day.

The weather was clear and bright. Freddie knew the Luftwaffe would not be making any day time raids this day – clear and easy sitting for the ground gunners. Smoke still hung in the distance; Freddie wondered if Mill Street had been battered again.

Stepping out onto the platform, he saw Mr Potter disappearing into the ticket office. "Mr Potter! Mr Potter!" he shouted.

"Good morning, my boy," Mr Potter responded. "Come on over," he continued.

"They won't be coming today, will they?"

"I shouldn't think so, my boy."

"Good! My mum needs a break."

"Bless you, Freddie – you're a good and thoughtful boy." After patting Freddie on the head, forgetting for a moment his head wound, "Now go and see Mrs Potter, she will be in the cottage somewhere, the kitchen most likely; ask her to put the kettle on. It won't be long before the Home Guard turn up to finish the track work, and they will need a cuppa before they start."

"Yes sir." Freddie was off and running, crossing the tracks again and darting inside the cottage.

"Wow! Slow down, my lovely, where's the fire?" Mrs Potter said, with a broad smile.

"Sorry. Mr Potter said the Home Guard will be coming, and wants the kettle on."

"Does he now!" she replied. "I shall have to have words with Mr Potter." Realising Freddie didn't understand the tone or inference in her voice, she said simply, "Yes, my lovely."

With that Freddie raced outside again, crossed the tracks and headed towards the ticket office. Passing it in a flash, he shouted, "Going to check the top section of the tracks."

"Steady then," Mr Potter answered.

Freddie slowed to a walk, making the most of his new responsibility. Feeling very important, he dropped from the platform and straddled the tracks, casting his eyes along the rails. Walking, headed bowed, eyes fixed to ground level, he noticed the signal box door open again, only marginally, but open nonetheless.

Hello, Freddie thought to himself. "Grace Bagworth! Are you in there again?" he shouted. He hadn't seen Grace for a couple of days.

No reply came from within.

Inside the signal box, the landing party raised their weapons, pointed in one direction and one direction only. All German gazes fixed on the slightly open door. Shriver cursed under his breath, passing the most disapproving glare at Schmidt, visually reprimanding him for this oversight.

Freddie started towards the door, suspecting nothing! Stepping over the iron tracks, he was only a matter of several feet away, when he was startled by a shout from the station.

"Private!" Sergeant Struthers stood bolt upright on the platform. Freddie turned and, seeing the sergeant, smiled and waved. "Hello, Sergeant," he called back.

The Home Guard had arrived and Freddie was happy and excited at the prospect of being able to help and tidy up his most favourite place in the world.

"At the double, Sergeant," he mocked.

But as Freddie returned his gaze to the signal box, he noticed something that shouldn't have been there, something which wasn't normal, something that clearly wasn't local. On the floor just to the right-hand side of the open signal box door, he saw a button! A silver-coloured button, and his eagle eyes had spied an emblem resembling an eagle. *What!* he thought.

Shining in the morning sunlight, the glitter and flash of reflections in the light had drawn his attention.

In utter amazement, Freddie saw a hand creep out into the light, fingers attempting to grasp the item.

"Sergeant!" Freddie turned and started to run, pleading with his brain to make his legs move faster. "Sergeant! Sergeant!" Fear gripped his face.

Hearing the shouting, Mr Potter emerged from the ticket office. Sergeant Struthers pinpointed his gaze on Freddie. Corporal Sam Burton and Private Billy Turpin, as if on a running track, set off at a sprint. All eyes focused in one direction.

At that same moment, the signal box door burst open. Shadowy figures appeared, crouching and kneeling and raising weapons to the ready. A number of figures dived to the ground to the left and right of the signal box, hitting the ground with a heavy thud, without showing any signs of discomfort.

Neither the German force nor the Home Guard were afforded any protective cover in that instant.

Sam Burton and Billy Turpin slid to a halt, their hobnailed boots scraping the concrete platform surface. Other members of the Home Guard, including Captain Siddlington-Brown, appeared, weapons, at the ready, unsure what was happening. However, they immediately had to duck for cover as a volley of bullets burst from the signal box.

"Get down, boy! Hit the deck!" Sergeant Struthers shouted to Freddie, even as he was diving for whatever cover he could find himself. In that split second it seemed like a war of a different kind had arrived in Liverpool. "Keep your head down, lad!" Struthers shouted.

"Sergeant! Sergeant, are you hit?" Captain Siddlington-Brown shouted.

"No!" came the reply.

"Burton, Turpin, what about you?"

"Okay, sir!"

"Sergeant, how many and their positions?" Captain Siddlington-Brown was unsighted from his current covering position.

"Numbers not known! Signal box at two o'clock. Looks like they are trying to outflank us, sir!"

Siddlington-Brown raised his head. He wanted to get 'eyes on' but his position didn't allow that. For the time being, Sergeant Struthers was his eyes and ears. From his position towards the end of the platform, he was currently out of the field of fire, with good observation.

"Burton. Any movement? And you have my permission to open fire."

"Thank you, sir!" a calm voice replied.

"Turpin! Crawl over here, man."

"Not likely, sir!" a less than calm voice replied.

"Get over here, man, I need the Vickers."

The Vickers was a rapid firing machine gun, first introduced and used by the British Army in 1912. It was water-cooled and usually had a three man crew to operate it. With a combined weight of between thirty-three and fifty-one pounds, a total gun length of three point eight inches and barrel length of twenty-eight inches, it had a muzzle velocity of two thousand four hundred and forty feet per second and was belt fed with a two hundred and fifty round capacity. It loaded quickly enough, it had the capability of firing between four hundred and fifty and five hundred rounds per minute; a very effective weapon.

Currently, the Toxteth Home Guard was one of only a handful of platoons to have one. It hadn't actually been fired yet and training in its usage was still being handed down to the rank and file in the platoon.

"Give me a minute, sir!" Private Turpin took a deep breath and placed his belly on the ground.

"Get a move on, man!"

"Yeah! Yeah!" Turpin muttered to himself, snaking his way from the cottage side of the station. As he did so, a new burst of gunfire burst overhead.

"Lay down cover fire!" Captain Siddlington-Brown shouted. "But don't waste ammunition," he continued.

"Don't waste ammo – good grief." Corporal Burton was thinking, this is a life and death situation! Directing the other members of the platoon, a volley was fired towards the German invaders.

Turpin rose to his feet and raced over the tracks, diving headlong onto the platform and rolling into the ticket office. Staying low, he gazed up to see Mr Potter crouched at the side of a metal filing cabinet.

"Nice of you to join us!" Potter said.

"Don't you start, too. What are my customers going to say, if they don't get their goods I promised them?"

"Last thing you should be worrying about, sonny."

"Hey, business is business!" Turpin knew that ladies were expecting nylons, the milkman was expecting horse food and spare parts for the milk float. "I didn't sign up for this," he went on.

"You didn't sign up at all, laddie!" Mr Potter said.

"Yeah! Yeah!" Shrugging, Turpin stated, "Well I'd better go for the Vickers, then!"

"Seems like a good idea," Potter quizzed.

Private Turpin bunny hopped to the side door and staying low edged his way out. The platoon van was parked near to this door which had a ramp access. This of course would help when he was wheeling the Vickers towards the platform.

Minutes later the Vickers gun, mounted on wheels for manoeuvrability, was in position, stationed at the ticket office door. Turpin was sweating heavily; the effort of wheeling the weapon into position on his own sapped his strength.

Placing the magazine in place, cocking the hammer, Turpin shouted, "Ready, Captain."

"Well point and fire the darn thing!" replied Siddlington-Brown.

"Right you are, sir."

Squeezing the trigger, the unmistakable sound of the weapon rattled a field of fire streaming down the platform and towards the occupied signal box. Turpin struggled to handle the weapon alone.

"Freddie!" Sergeant Struthers shouted. "Get up and run to me!"

The hailstorm of .303 rounds directed at the signal box splintered the oak frame as if made of balsa wood. The German landing party buried their heads. "Now, Freddie!" shouted Sergeant Struthers.

"Now son, run!"

Freddie Bloom picked himself up and ran for his life. "Come on, son, come on!" Struthers urged the boy to run like the wind. At the same time Corporal Sam Burton jumped from the platform, took a prone position and fired. His bolt action .303 Lee Enfield rang out. "Go on son!" he thought out loud.

Struthers manhandled Freddie onto the platform and behind the cover used as his observation point. "Good boy." A beaming smile seemed to fill his whole face.

When the Vickers paused, the Nazi invaders returned fire, small arms only. They had been compromised; to all intents and purposes their mission had failed. Their aim now was to evade capture for as long as possible, and when all was lost, they were to fight to the death!

"Schmidt. Fall back to the RV point," Oberleutnant Shriver ordered.

"Yes sir!" came the reply.

"I will give cover fire. You must get the information back to the U-boat! Do you understand? At all costs!"

"Sir!" Schmidt gave instant obedience.

The Vickers burst into life again. Billy Turpin had reloaded, laying down a barrage of fire, spitting wood, stone, track ballast, anything in its path, skywards.

In the mayhem, all but Oberleutnant Wilhelm Shriver crawled away, shifting their position to the rear of the signal box. Their way was clear back to the river. In defiance, Shriver continued to play out small arms fire.

Tapping on a transmitter, a coded message began making its way across the airwaves. Its destination was U-534.

"Privates, go right." Captain Siddlington-Brown pointed to the remaining members of the platoon. "Cover the rear."

Another burst from the Vickers.

"Come on, you filthy Hun!" Turpin shouted, trying to be heard above the rattling Vickers. "See what Billy has for you," he went on.

Another burst rang out.

"Potter, Potter!" Billy Turpin shouted. "Get the other belts from the truck, running low out here." The heat from the Vickers barrel, sending up vapour mixing with the gunsmoke, made it look like a sudden mist had descended. *Glad this thing is water-cooled!* he thought.

"Will do, laddie," Potter responded.

"Captain! Captain!" Billy couldn't hear his own voice. "Captain!" "What?" A surprisingly calm voice came through.

"Sir, I'm running low on ammo, Potter has gone for more. Going to need some cover here!" Turpin ceased firing, so lowered his voice.

"Understood." Turning to Corporal Burton, "Corporal, take a position near the ticket office."

"Do my best, Captain," Sam Burton replied.

"Has anyone thought of calling headquarters?" Siddlington-Brown asked.

"Yes sir, message sent and they said, "Hold at all cost." Siddlington-Brown couldn't remember his name, but thanked him anyway.

The Nazi raiders regrouped at the rear of the signal box. Schmidt hurled a grenade stick down the tracks. "Oberleutnant! This way."

Another grenade stick was thrown, and another, and another.

"Grenades!" Struthers screamed.

Three consecutive explosions filled the air. Smoke billowed from ground level, the perfect cover for their senior officer.

"Quickly, Oberleutnant, this way."

More small arms fire erupted.

Keeping low, Oberleutnant Shriver hurried himself back towards the signal box. His men had served him well, creating a smoke screen for him to make his escape.

He used the smoke well.

Shrapnel exploded in all directions as the once dormant grenade sticks burst into their deadly life.

By the time the Home Guard raised their heads again, the signal box was empty. The raiders had vanished.

"Quickly men, check it out." Captain Siddlington-Brown ordered the assault on the box. "Cover them, Turpin."

Draping another sling across the Vickers and cocking the heavy gun, it was trained on the signal box once more. The scene was quiet now, the smoke clearing. The box door was wide open, the surrounding wooden panels strafed with .303 rounds. The Vickers had gone through it like a knife through butter.

"Clear!"

"Clear!"

"Clear here!"

One by one the Home Guard reported the signal box and the rear were clear. "Good," responded Captain Siddlington-Brown. "Sergeant, roll call, please."

"Sir." Sergeant Struthers commenced a name tally of the guard. "All present, sir, no injury to report."

"Excellent," he went on. "Mr Potter, how are things?"

"Well enough, Captain," came the reply.

Corporal Billy Turpin retraced his steps and then back to the railway cottage. Mrs Potter and Mrs Bloom emerged, both unscathed. Shocked for sure, but unhurt.

"Freddie! Freddie!" Mrs Bloom screamed. "He's fine, Mrs Bloom. He's right over there." Billy Turpin pointed towards the end of the platform.

Sergeant Struthers appeared with Freddie, both unscathed.

"My God, you were lucky there, young man. Are you sure you're okay?" Struthers was concerned, this was not a war for boys.

"I'm okay, really," Freddie pointed to all parts of his body. "See, no holes!"

Jogging along the platform, Freddie headed towards his mother. He could see she was crying; more in relief now than anything else.

"You silly boy!" she shouted.

"Mum! That was great."

"Don't you dare say that, you silly boy." She grabbed him and held him so tight. She wasn't really angry, it was raw emotion kicking in. He could have been killed. She could have lost her other son.

Chapter Seven

Lying deep in the Irish Sea, U-534 was in a state of full readiness; dim red lights throughout the boat, hushed voices and worried faces.

Kapitan Nollau paced the command centre – no word from the landing party. *This is not good,* he thought. He continually stepped into the radio room, adjacent to the control room. "Any contact yet?" he asked.

"Not yet, Kapitan."

"Any shipping contact?"

"No, Kapitan."

His gaze moved to the Enigma machine positioned next to the radio operator. It was silent!

"We should have heard by now," he said, but the radio operator didn't think he required a response. The landing party was now some two hours overdue. The longer U-534 was on station, the greater the risk of detection. The whole mission may have been compromised; at worst, it may have failed completely. He had no way of knowing.

His orders were strictly no contact from the boat. He was duty bound to await the contact from Oberleutnant Wilhelm Shriver; the matter was totally in his hands.

Another hour passed and still no contact from shore. Just like the landing, the extraction was to be completed during the hours of darkness. If U-534 surfaced in daylight, she would surely never make it out in one piece.

However, daybreak was now well on the way.

"Any message?" he said, in a muted but firm if somewhat hesitant voice, to the radio room.

"There was a very brief signal, but it's gone now, Kapitan," came the reply.

"Did you get any of it?"

"No, sir."

"Damn!" Nollau sounded dejected, angry and frustrated – every negative emotion possible.

Klaus Hoffmann brought a mug of coffee to his kapitan. "Sir – time is critical."

"Yes! Yes!" Nollau responded, annoyance in his voice.

"We have to make a decision, Kapitan. We cannot stay here much longer."

"I am well aware of that, Hoffmann," running his fingers through his greying hair. "We stay."

"Sir! Contact bearing 250!" The radio operator could not disguise the anguish in his voice.

"Rig the boat," shouted the kapitan.

"Aye, sir," Hoffmann responded immediately. "Silence in the boat."

Crew in the control room hurried to different stations – levers altered, panels starting to flash with red lights, which after several seconds turned green.

"Boat rigged, sir," Hoffmann shouted.

"Take her deep," ordered Nollau.

"Make depth one five zero, silent running."

Ten seconds later, "Depth now one five zero feet," the helmsman reported.

"All stop," said Nollau.

"All stop, sir, aye."

The crew obeyed like clockwork, no-one moved inside the boat. No voices were heard. The slightest sound would be instantly detected on the active sonar above, searching. The Royal Navy made regular sweeps of the river mouth and out into the Irish Sea. After all this was war. The Royal Navy would never take anything for granted.

"Contact now two thousand yards and closing," the sonar operator reported.

Seconds later, the same voice whispered, "Contact now one thousand seven hundred and seventy-five yards."

Beads of sweat were trickling down the face of the cornered kapitan.

Pressing his headphones tight to his ears, the sonar operator blocked everything else out; his sole attention was on the 'ping' in his ears. His immediate concern was to attempt to identify the oncoming ship. This would assist his kapitan in the small matter of how he would evade and escape the warship. It clearly was a warship, heading straight to their position.

"Have they located us?" Nollau whispered. "Or is this routine?"

"Not sure yet, sir."

"I want to know any course change, understand?"

"Aye, sir."

His thoughts moved to the prospect of hearing depth charges pinging in his ears.

"It's a destroyer, sir. Four screws."

"Course change?" said Nollau.

"Stand by."

"Rig for depth charge," Nollau ordered.

"Aye, sir."

After what seemed an age, the sonar operator called out, "Contact now bearing two-fifty to one thousand yards."

Interrupting the sonar man, the radio operator burst in. "Sir, message received."

"Damn!" Nollau muttered.

"Kapitan – sonar. Contact is British V-Class battleship."

The ship causing all the concern was HMS Prince of Wales, or PoW as she was known to her crew.

She was a formidable foe; limited in size due to new construction regulations, she was around thirty-five thousand tons. Her size did not detract from her fire power – four ten inch main guns, two mounted in forward turrets and one mounted aft. These were her main attack weapons.

In her defence, she had sixteen 5.25 guns, thirty-two two pounder pom-pom cannons and sixteen 12.7mm (.50 calibre) anti-aircraft guns. She was also in possession of two Supermarine Walrus amphibious aircraft, used for general patrolling and search and rescue. These were launched via two double-ended catapults mounted amidships.

She was powered by four Parsons geared turbines, which were fed by eight superheated boilers, allowing her to achieve a credible surface speed of twenty-eight knots. As an addition she had recently been fitted with two depth charge launchers mounted aft.

The Prince of Wales happened to be in the Irish Sea at this time by pure chance; she was awaiting her orders to transport Churchill to an Atlantic meeting with President Roosevelt in Newfoundland.

This was to be ahead of her eventual fate; she later became involved in the titanic battle with the German powerhouse the Bismarck. In unison with HMS Hood, they engaged the Bismarck, inflicting direct hits on the ship.

The resulting damage forced the Bismarck to steam towards Brest for repairs.

The Princes of Wales later went on to be stationed in the Pacific and, after being torpedoed by the Japanese in 1941, it took only one hour twenty minutes for her to go down with all hands.

Her brief involvement in World War Two was memorable and assured her place in history. However, her loss and those who served aboard her will never be forgotten.

Her late commander, Captain Leach, would make history this day too.

"What about the message?" Nollau shouted. No need to whisper now.

"Broken off, sir."

"Range five hundred yards."

"Left full rudder!" Nollau shouted. Silent running was now out of the question.

"All ahead full."

"Aye sir."

The sonar was now ringing out over the boat's speaker system. All the crew knew there was a massive warship bearing down on them. Would they survive this day?

"Did you get any of it?" Nollau wanted to know if the landing party were coming back.

"Only part of a message, sir. 'Intel gained, stop, compromised, stop.' That's all I got, sir."

"Three hundred yards and closing, sir," the sonar interrupted.

"Right full rudder," Nollau bellowed.

"Right full rudder, aye, sir."

The two helmsmen battled with the rudder controls. Kapitan Nollau was now playing a game of cat and mouse, knowing he could turn quicker than his pursuer.

"Depth two zero zero," he ordered.

"Aye, sir."

The sonar echo was ear-piercingly loud now, she was right on top of them.

"Left full rudder!" Nollau barked out again.

The sonar operator suddenly alerted the kapitan. "Depth charges in the water."

"Brace for impact!" shouted Nollau.

"Another depth charge in the water."

"And another one, sir."

"And… and another one, Kapitan."

"Steady man," Nollau tried to reassure.

Silence. Then the next ten seconds were like hell being unleashed. Four rapid explosions violently rocked the boat. Valves and pipes gave way, sea water started rushing inside the boat, sailors turning knobs and pushing levers, trying to stem the flow of water.

Lights dimmed and burst into life again, water continued spitting on the crew in the control room. Then lights exploded, as water shorted them.

The loudspeaker still thundered with the propulsion system of the Princes of Wales, interrupted only when the engine room burst through. "Kapitan – we're taking on water!"

"Aye. Seal the bulkheads." Nollau was alarmed and that showed in his voice; he was aware that his boat may not see the day out. "Seal the bulkheads," he shouted again. The noise in the control room was horrific.

"Another one in the water, sir," sonar reported.

"Three more, Kapitan," he went on.

"Brace! Brace! Brace!" Nollau shouted.

U-534, shock out of control, the charges exploded in what seemed like a single earth-moving boom.

"We have lost control, sir!" shouted the helmsmen in unison.

The boat was going down. "Power gone," came a voice on the loudspeaker.

Chapter Eight

"Oberleutnant! Still no response from the U-boat."

The landing party had taken refuge in a dockland warehouse packed with wooden crates and boxes. They had escaped the attention of the Home Guard at the railway station, without any loss.

They were now dangerously low on ammunition, and their means of total escape was out of contact.

"Check the Enigma, Franz."

"It is working, sir." he replied.

"We may have to make our stand here; post the men. I want one there, covering the main entrance. Another there in the gantry, covering the entrance; both positions should lay down a good field of fire." Shriver gave the orders and he expected each man to fight to the last.

"Check and secure an escape route, if there is one."

"Yes, sir." Franz Schmidt said. He saluted and left, shouting orders to two others. "You two, with me."

As of this point, their mission was a disaster. They had failed to obtain any significant movement information. They learned nothing which would benefit any invasion. In fact, they hadn't even been able to move more than three and a half miles from their landing point.

Shriver could see his career going down the drain; however, he was stuck with it and his aim now was purely survival. He would face the backlash should he leave these shores alive; at the moment that was indeed in doubt.

These thoughts were immaterial at the present, he alone was aware of the conditions of this mission. His orders were to fight to the death – a fact he had not yet conveyed to his men.

To pick the right time to tell them? Would there be a right time?

It was only a matter of time before the real military force arrived and not the bunch of ageing men he faced earlier. As a soldier, though, he had respect for the Home Guard. He had clearly underestimated their capabilities and certainly their weaponry. He had not been given information that they would be armed with a Vickers machine gun.

But that was the past. He needed to focus, use his experience and training to at least achieve something; to sink a ship in port would be some consolation.

"Men in position, sir," said Schmidt.

"Thank you, Franz."

"We have located an escape route overhead. We should be able to move from warehouse to warehouse, using the skylights; we would need to leave someone here for covering fire and to continue the deception, whilst the rest slip away."

The Oberleutnant didn't like the sound of leaving a man behind, but it may be the only way.

"Let's play it by ear, Franz," Shriver said, patting him on the shoulder; looking at his radio operator, "Keep trying to get something through."

"Yes, sir."

Chapter Nine

Janet Bloom held her son so tight, relieved that nothing had happened to him. He could have easily been shot, there at the station.

"There dear, he's fine – see!" said Mrs Potter.

"Now, young Freddie," Mr Potter said, running his hands over Freddie's body, checking for bullet holes. Although he was trying to look and sound calm, Mr Potter had feared the worst. Bullets flying everywhere – anything could have happened.

Captain Siddlington-Brown ran across the platform. "Any sign of them, Sergeant?" his voice excited.

"The lads are out in the streets now, sir. They can't have got that far," Sergeant Struthers responded.

"What a damn mess!" came the reply.

"I tried to warn everyone, Mr Potter, honest I did," Freddie said.

"I know lad, I know." He put his round around Freddie. "Don't worry about it, the army and Home Guard will track them down. You did well, my boy."

The local police and regular military were now buzzing around Dingle station. Patrols were out on the streets, road blocks and check points had been set up and secured.

The military brass strutted round the station, armed guards were in position, and it looked like Captain Siddlington-Brown was receiving a dressing down for his handling of the situation.

Mr Potter shepherded Freddie away. "Come on, this is not for us."

"Captain, you have made a complete duck's arse of this altogether. I have never seen such a diabolical cock-up in the whole of my military service. You had better hope we get these infiltrators soonest, or you will be hung out to dry, mark my words!" Major Plaistow was not a man to be trifled with; a long service soldier who had seen conflict around the world, a junior officer during the latter stages of the First World War, quickly rising through the ranks. He did not suffer fools!

"Yes, sir," Siddlington-Brown responded.

"Get out of my sight, man!" Major Plaistow bellowed.

Snapping a salute, Siddlington-Brown completed an about turn and briskly marched the length of the platform. The embarrassment on his face was clear to see.

"You men! What are you doing there with your fingers up your arses? Get out there and find those Nazis!" Plaistow was almost bursting blood vessels in his face and neck.

The Home Guard soldiers he was referring to turned on their heels and quick marched in the opposite direction; any direction as long as it was away from the Major. They quickly exited the station to street level.

Captain Siddlington-Brown was already outside, licking his wounds. When his men approached, rather sheepishly he said, "Well, men, seems the Major is none too pleased! For what it's worth, I consider your actions, all your actions, to have been of the highest calibre in the face of the enemy. I was proud of each of you."

He went on. "If we had not been here at the time, the Germans would have overrun the station, gathered as much information as they could without being disturbed, and disappeared into the shadows again. They could have operated here for weeks, months. Who knows how many people in this city may have died as a result."

He was not a man with whom the rest of the platoon would have socialised in normal situations, but they did feel for him that day. He had taken a verbal beating from a ranking officer and taken it in good form. They respected him now for that.

"Sir, give us the order! Where would you like us to deploy?" Sergeant Struthers barked out.

"Thank you, Sergeant," Captain Siddlington-Brown answered.

"We need to find them, and quickly, just to shove it up the Major," Struthers offered.

"That's enough, Sergeant. I won't tolerate any disrespect, even if it's well-intended," Siddlington-Brown countered. After a pause, he went on, "Gather the platoon on Park Road, we'll have our own debrief."

"Will do, sir."

Freddie was excited, telling his mum everything that had happened. For him it was like a Boys Own adventure. Fighting the Hun on English soil, repelling the invaders – although they hadn't been repelled – for the time being, they had just disappeared.

"Calm down, Freddie," Mrs Bloom said.

"Now Mrs Bloom, let the boy enjoy his story. He is a local hero now, you know," Mr Potter said; at the same time a beaming smile crossed his face. He winked at Mrs Potter.

"Yeah mum! A hero!" he said.

"Whatever next?" Mrs Potter offered.

"Can I go and tell Grace, Mum?"

"Well, only if you are sure you are okay?"

"Course I am." Freddie didn't even wait for the answer, he was off and running, out of the station onto Park Street and up the hill to Park Road, running beyond the Home Guard and waving as he did so.

"A Platoon, secure the warehouses. B Platoon, secure the dock road as far as the Strand," Major Plaistow ordered. Full-time soldiers were now taking charge of this unfortunate situation.

From their hiding place in the warehouse, Oberleutnant Shriver was aware that the net may well be closing, and their initial escape may be short-lived. "Sir, men in position," Schmidt said.

"Try the Enigma again," Shriver said.

A coded message was again sent, for the third time. The operator waited, and waited. "Nothing, Oberleutnant."

Shriver was deeply concerned now. It had been many hours since their scheduled pick-up, and to make matters worse, now U 534 wasn't responding.

This may be the time to tell the men what was expected of them by the German High Command. In his own mind Shriver knew he alone would be the only man not to leave – he would do his very best to get his men back out to sea. They would not suffer because they survived, they would only state they were acting under orders.

If nothing else, German generals believed in obeying orders – to the letter. It would only be Shriver's family who would suffer any humiliation; if he were to survive.

Aboard HMS Prince of Wales, Captain Leach had his ship lurching from port to starboard at speed, responding to the directional changes from the sonar operator. He knew he had the U-boat in his sights and he wasn't going to let her escape. She was there for the taking.

Through the hand held radio, "Port charges – fire!" He watched from the bridge, as one after another four high explosive depth charges rose skyward, before falling and splashing beneath the waves.

"Hard-a-starboard," he ordered, and she immediately responded, waves crashing over the bow. "Ready, starboard charges." Seconds later, "Fire!"

The Prince had turned on herself and laid down yet another barrage of explosive doom. Four more splashes, followed by a further four explosions.

U-534 was listing sharply to stern. She violently shook again, taking on water from aft ballast tanks; it seemed her fate was already sealed. No matter what Kapitan Nollau did, she was going down. Her crew were hanging on to whatever they could to prevent themselves from spiralling along the boat.

"Blow all tanks," Nollau ordered.

The noise inside now was intense, men screaming like babies. Sea water rushed in, sparks crackling from the electric cables, everyone trying to shout above everyone else. The scene was chaotic.

"Flood the escape hatches!" Kapitan Nollau shouted.

"Fire!" The words echoed in the weapons' controllers headphones. Pushing the palm of his hand against the fire button, more depth charges were released. More splashes, more explosions.

"Hard-a-port." Captain Leach spoke calmly into the microphone. The ship slew round, the foredeck awash, the raging waters around the Prince of Wales boiled with anger, a white mass of superheated froth.

"All stop."

"Aye. All stop."

"Lookouts, please." Leach wanted confirmation the last explosion was in fact the U-boat imploding. "Report any debris."

"Raft in the water, bearing two four zero degrees." The foreward lookout pointed.

"XO, launch the RIB," the Captain said.

"Aye, sir."

"Man the .50 cal.," he went on.

The foreward lookout pointed again. "Sir, second raft in the water."

Midship's lookout spoke. "Debris in the water.

Placing the binoculars to his face, Captain Leach scanned the sea. He noted unused life jackets, in sight then disappearing and reappearing again between the waves, oil lying on the surface, pieces of wood and torn-away clothing. It was evident the U-boat had imploded. It also appeared that the sole survivors were those sprawled in the rafts. Only two rafts were visible on the surface.

Speaking to his XO via radio link, "Keep searching."

"Aye, sir."

The Princes of Wales continued circling as Captain Leach watched the rescue RIBs in the water. Medical staff was ready to receive the survivors.

Chapter Ten

Arriving on Park Road, Freddie bounded up the sandstone front steps and knocked at the door of 195.

He couldn't wait to tell Grace everything. Finding the Germans, the gun fight and how he was nearly shot. His mind raced recalling the events. It really felt like he was actually a soldier.

The front door opened. Mrs Bagworth stood in front of him. "Hello, Freddie."

"Hello Mrs Bagworth. Is Grace at home?"

"Come in and I'll call her."

Stepping through the door, Freddie wiped his feet on the door mat – it was polite.

Moments later Grace appeared at the top of the stairs and bounded down them two at a time.

"Hiya, Freddie."

"Grace! I've got so much to tell you."

They sat in the back parlour, Freddie going through as much as he could remember. Even Mrs Bagworth was seated and listening intently.

"Oh, my word!" she said.

"How exciting, Freddie." Grace was sad that she had missed it all.

Hardly bearing to tear herself from the story, Mrs Bagworth moved to the back kitchen and poured a small glass of lemonade, and hurried back to the parlour. Freddie stopped as she entered.

"Please go on, Freddie. What happened next?" she asked.

Freddie was really enjoying the spotlight, he was feeling more and more like hero. He told them of the shoot-out, the grenades exploding, the Vickers gun tearing through the signal box – a place Grace had been not too long before.

Freddie was very descriptive with his account.

Chapter Eleven

Dockers had been evacuated from the warehouse area. They hadn't argued about it; a fire fight now raged at the warehouses. Explosions and continuous rapid weapon fire filled the air, fires breaking out, thick black smoke billowed up, almost turning day into night.

Major Plaistow barked his orders. There was no way in hell that he was going to let these German invaders walk away from this. His hard-hitting attitude hadn't always gone down well with his superiors. His out-spoken and self-opinionated thoughts often proved unpopular with higher ranks.

Today he would prove a point!

Plaistow had deployed his platoons of regulars, unaware that Captain Siddlington-Brown and the volunteers had followed the sounds of the fire fight.

Local knowledge was now to play a part.

Captain Siddlington-Brown was born in the Kensington area of the city and had never lived anywhere other than Liverpool; a born and bred Scouser, if only from the posh part of the city.

He knew the city like the back of his hand and, almost as importantly, he knew the men from his volunteer platoon were also born and bred Scousers. An advantage the regulars didn't have.

"Okay chaps! Options?" Siddlington-Brown spoke softly.

"Sir. One, the Nazis must have a boat somewhere. Unless it's a suicide mission, they will be wanting to leave. Two, best place to re-join their boat? Three, they tough it out down at the docks and no-one leaves!" Sergeant Struthers offered his thoughts.

"Agreed. Thank you, Sergeant," Siddlington-Brown responded. "Clearly this is only a small raiding party. We know they are cornered, we also can assume that they are hard and seasoned soldiers…"

Private Bill Turpin interrupted him. "Bloody marvellous!"

"Yes, thank you, Turpin, that's enough of that!" Siddlington-Brown verbally rapped him. "Now! If I were in their shoes, I would head for the Albert Dock." He paused for comment. His Home Guard boys just looked on. "The Admiralty requisitioned the Dock to control the Atlantic Fleet from there. What's more, even subs used it and some are there now. A landing boat would be a way the Nazis can escape to sea!"

"Nice one, Cap." Corporal Sam Burton voiced his agreement.

"Thanks, Burton! Right, Sergeant Struthers, you take the men to Albert Dock, deploy the Vickers. I'll report to the Major and meet you there."

"Sir," Struthers answered. "Right you lot, on me. Let's move!"

"Be careful, men." Siddlington-Brown stated the obvious.

The fire fight was still raging in the warehouses along the Duke's Dock, which is located south of Albert Dock. Major Plaistow had the enemy pinned down, his men continuing to lay down a massive field of fire.

Oberleutnant Wilhelm Shriver had asked for volunteers to remain behind and keep the fire fight going. Every one of his men took a step forward. Sergeant Franz Schmidt had chosen one other to remain – all extra ammunition was left for the pair. They had to give the impression that the British were still facing a heavily armed band of invaders, whilst the escape was put into operation.

Chapter Twelve

Freddie had recounted the whole story and how the events unfolded to Grace. He was excited and speaking at a pace that would have been comparable with the firing rate of the Vickers machine gun. Grace was struggling to keep up.

"Come on!" he shouted to Grace.

"Where?"

"The docks, where else? Can't you hear the firing?"

"No way!" she said.

"We have to, we have to see the Germans when they surrender. Come on."

"I'm not sure about that, Freddie!" Mrs Bagworth suggested.

Mrs Bagworth didn't want the children in harm's way; she told Grace not to go and Freddie agreed that they wouldn't.

"We will stay up this end," Freddie reassured her.

With that Freddie was off, tugging Grace along with him. They headed from Park Road onto Parliament Street; turning left they headed towards the waterfront, the gun battle getting louder now.

"But you told my mum we wouldn't!" Grace said.

"I know! But we have to see the Hun captured, don't we?"

Passing Wapping Dock, they headed towards Salthouse Dock and Salthouse Quay. Freddie was fully aware that the navy ships docked at Albert Dock and that there would be soldiers and sailors there. As they passed over a metal walkway across Wapping Dock, Freddie heard a familiar voice.

"Over here, lad!" Sergeant Struthers called out to the pair. "Freddie, get over here now!"

"Sergeant!" Freddie sounded surprised.

"Where the hell do you think you are going?"

"We wanted to see the Germans captured."

"Not yet my lad, can't you hear the fighting?"

"Yeah, I can." Freddie was excited. The war seemed a lot closer today.

"And you brought young Grace with you! What are you thinking of?" Struthers sounded angry.

Sergeant Struthers grabbed his shoulder and pulled him to cover. Billy Turpin took a less forceful hold on Grace and moved her to safe cover; he gave her a wink with his left eye.

"What on earth are you two scallies doing down here?" Private Turpin asked.

"It was his idea!" said Grace.

"Well, my girl, it wasn't the best idea Freddie ever had. It's dangerous, if you hadn't noticed."

The Home Guard had taken up a position on the south side of Albert Dock, close to Salthouse Quay. Strategically the platoon had a full field of fire on Albert Dock should the enemy attempt to take one of the boats moored.

The Admiralty guard were on full alert; Sergeant Struthers had fully briefed the commanding officer. The dock defences were as usual fully manned and anti-aircraft batteries encased by sandbags were fully operational. Machine gun posts were armed and ready, positioned behind double layered sandbags which would stop small arms penetration.

Freddie saw six or more landing boats moored to the quay, a grey outline of a warship; he had no idea of her name. Fortunately there were no submarines present this day.

"For God's sake, Freddie, keep your head down!" Struthers shouted at him. The Home Guard had been designated, due to their initial involvement in the events, to provide the first line of defence, or attack if required. Sandbags were hurriedly gathered and positioned three feet high on the south entrance to Albert Dock, the Vickers gun in prime location.

"Freddie! What the blazes?" Captain Siddlington-Brown had just arrived and couldn't believe his eyes. "Young Grace, you too?"

Before Freddie could say anything, Sergeant Struthers interrupted. "As strange as it seems, sir, young Freddie here had the same idea as you! That the Nazis would try to make for the escape route using one of our own landing boats."

"Umm!" was the only response.

Before any further conversation, the air burst into flashes of blinding light, ear-piercing claps of thunderous noise. It all seemed so close.

"Get down!" Siddlington-Brown yelled. "Who's on the Vickers?"

"Sam," Sergeant Struthers answered.

"Burton, open her up, man."

"Yes sir!" Sam Burton needed no further orders. Cocking the impressive weapon, the sheer noise was deafening, red hot flames breathing from the muzzle as round after round cannoned towards the enemy.

Freddie and Grace slammed their hands to their ears; the Vickers, only a matter of feet away, thrashed into the enemy positions, although at this stage they hadn't really pinpointed the Nazi attackers, general firing, laying down suppressing fire.

"Short bursts, Burton, short bursts only!" Siddlington-Brown ordered.

When Corporal Burton ceased fire, it was quiet – no incoming fire!

"Spin slowly round to the west, Burton," Capt. Siddlington-Brown whispered. The dock was in darkness, all eyes scanned for some, any movement – there was none.

In the direction of Dukes Dock, the fighting appeared to have slowed and was more sporadic now. Siddlington-Brown had advised Major Plaistow that he thought the Germans would make a run for it, and that was what now appeared to be happening. The Major, however, was not impressed; being told or advised by the Home Guard did not sit very well and he had dismissed the notion.

The Captain had not argued, he had just stated his thoughts and left. He wanted to join his platoon a.s.a.p.

The Home Guard waited, the Admiralty guard waited. An eerie silence now descended around Albert Dock. Lights remained off, no-one spoke, eyes peered, scanning any movement. It seemed all fighting had stopped.

Some shouting could be heard from the Dukes Dock area, but the words were not distinguishable. The Captain gestured his finger to his lips, wanting silence from his men.

By the time Sergeant Struthers looked back, Freddie and Grace had gone. "Where the hell?" Struthers whipped his head left and then right; the two young ones were nowhere to be seen. "Captain, a problem!"

"What now, Sergeant? I don't need more problems at the moment!"

"You want to know this, sir."

"Okay, let's hear it," he said, without looking back, his eyes still focused on the potential killing area ahead of him.

"Well… it's eh!"

"Spit it out man! What's the problem?"

After a pause, Sergeant Struthers said, "Okay! Freddie and young Grace have gone! I don't know where."

Turning in a flash, "What? Damn it, Sergeant – they were your responsibility."

"I know, sir, I'm sorry. One minute they were here, the next, gone!"

"Find them, Sergeant, now!"

"Sir."

In the silence Freddie had noticed figures moving in the shadows, ducking and hiding between short movements. He had assumed that this would not have been the Home Guard or even the British regular soldiers; it had to be the Germans. Figures edging towards Albert Dock and the boats moored there.

Having no chance to tell his friend, Sergeant Struthers, he knew he had to follow and keep these figures in sight, without being seen himself. He had tugged Grace along with him, raising his right hand to her face, "Shoosh!"

Creeping out beyond the stacked sandbags, Freddie and Grace watched, peered into the darkness, trying to follow every movement. He whispered to Grace, "They are going for a boat." After a moment, Freddie said, "Wait here, Grace, I'm going over there." He pointed to a low stone wall running along Salthouse Quay, from where he would have a clear view of the dock and in particular the landing crafts.

Grace did what she was told, her heart was racing, and fear gripped her whole body. Freddie now disappeared into the darkness.

Searchlights now bathed Albert Dock in pinpoint beams of light, the Admiralty guards desperate to locate the invading Nazis. They could not fail; they had to be found. The lights continued hopping across the water and around the dock.

This only served to heighten the panic Grace was feeling.

Chapter Thirteen

"Mr Potter, have you seen Freddie? He should have been back from Grace's house a while ago." Mrs Bloom had urgency in her voice, not to mention fear.

"I haven't, my dear." Mr Potter checked his fob watch. It was indeed late now, too late for young Freddie to be out, in light of events. "Where was he going?"

"To Park Road, where Grace lives."

"Stay calm now, I will go round and make enquiries. You stay with Mrs Potter."

Not awaiting a reply, Mr Potter strode off, away from the railway station, heading towards Park Road, which fortunately wasn't too far away, just a few streets.

Mrs Bagworth had no idea where they were.

"You go to the station and wait there, I will find them both," Mr Potter tried to reassure her.

Park Road was negative; no sign of Freddie and even more troubling, young Grace was missing too. Standing in the middle of Park Road, station master Potter stroked the back of his neck, his concern was clearly evident. *Where are you?* he thought.

His thoughts were interrupted when he was approached by a sole ARP warden.

"Mr Potter! What are you doing up here?"

Without any greeting, Potter said, "Looking for young Freddie Bloom and Grace Bagworth from that house there." He pointed to the house on Park Road. "They're missing somewhere. Have you seen either of them?"

"Sorry, no!"

"Damn!" said Potter.

"I take it you heard about the Jerry? The word is they are being engaged by our boys down at the docks." The warden nodded as he walked off.

Mr Potter gave a wry smile; of course he had heard about Jerry, he had been involved in events at the station.

"Better get off the street, Mr Potter, word is the Luftwaffe are on their way!" he shouted back over his shoulder.

The station master now knew for certain where Freddie was – he would have gone down to the docks. *I should have guessed!* he thought to himself. *Damn foolish little boy.*

Setting off at a sprint, Mr Potter headed towards the docks. He was just hoping he could find them both before they got themselves into any real trouble. He could hear the firing from that direction. He didn't much fancy going there, but he knew he had to.

Chapter Fourteen

The crew of HMS Prince of Wales were engaged in hauling survivors from the sea. Only two life rafts had broken the surface when U-534 had imploded; assumed to have imploded.

Thick fuel oil ladened the surface water; clothing, sections of wood and some personal items bobbed in the moderate swell. Six survivors only were plucked from the water, with blackened faces, charred clothing and none wearing footwear.

The rafts had been secured to the Prince's deck and the German submariners had been spread-eagled face down on the wooden deck and searched, then hands bound. No weapons.

The ship's medics gave them a quick once over. None was seriously injured; minor cuts and burns. It would be safe to secure them in the brig.

"Prisoners secure, sir."

"Thanks you, Number One." Captain Leach had positioned himself at the outer rail on the bridge, binoculars firmly to his eyes, the chilled air slapping the sides of his face.

"Seems we got them, Captain."

"Umm! Let's hope so, Number One." The captain wasn't sure or certain. It was an old submariner's trick to fake destruction, pumping items and oil out through the torpedo tubes, whilst playing possum on the sea bed.

A submarine often survived by playing dead. This was a tactic deployed throughout the war; sometimes it worked, sometimes it didn't.

"Let's make sure, Number One. Sweep the area again!"

"Yes, sir."

"I want to make absolutely sure we got them."

"Understood, sir."

Picking up the intercom Captain Leach spoke calmly and with confidence. "Chief! This is the Captain."

"Chief aye, go ahead sir," Chief Petty Officer William Howard answered.

"Chief, I want the prisoners interrogated now, understood? Over."

"Understood, sir."

"I want to know how badly the boat was damaged, understood? Over."

"Aye, sir. Chief out."

Replacing the binoculars to his face, Captain Leach was even more uncertain. This U-boat could still have a sting in the tail.

"Captain – sonar?"

"Sonar, aye."

"Anything?"

"Negative, Captain."

"Keep on your toes. Captain out."

Returning inside the bridge, Leach instructed the helmsmen to initiate defensive zigzag pattern.

"Let's take no chances, Number One."

Chapter Fifteen

Oberleutnant Shriver was within touching distance of the landing crafts at Albert Dock. Lurking in the shadows, he realised he was so close now, but with still a mammoth task ahead; seize a boat, get out of the dock and RV with his U-boat kapitan, or at least for his men to execute their escape. He was unaware that U-534 had been detected and engaged.

Shriver and his team had been on the run now for almost seven hours. He was certain two of his men would not be joining him, they would give their lives for the cause. For that reason alone, Shriver knew he must succeed, his crew must exit British waters and reach safe haven, report directly to his superiors. They alone would provide the information which could shorten the war and ultimate German victory.

His own future was not as positive.

He genuinely believed this. A product of the Hitler Youth, he had been indoctrinated with German supremacy. Adolf Hitler was viewed as a god at home. The Fuhrer was himself a veteran of the Great War, a decorated soldier who, post 1918, rose quickly through the ranks in government.

Hitler demanded respect; he was a cruel and vicious man if respect wasn't shown.

Failure to get his men to safety was not an option for Oberleutnant Shriver. After receiving his orders, he had made his own mind up. His men would not be sacrificed at any cost. If he fought to the death so be it; but not his men.

He knew the penalties for failure. Should he survive, he would be dealt with harshly, to say the least. If he lived through his interrogation the Russian front would undoubtedly be his final destination, together with complete humiliation for him and his family. They would be outcasts.

Hushed voices only broke the silence, the fighting from the warehouse had ceased. Shriver was clearly aware now that either his rear guard were dead, or eluding the British. Whichever – he had been given time to get the rest to a position of escape.

He had already written a letter commending his comrades for their courage and bravery in this mission, which had been left with a trusted friend back home. It would be presented to the High Command upon notification of his demise.

Edging closer to the quayside, Shriver issued 'hand only' commands to his team, instructing them forward, but slowly. Using whatever cover was available, the invaders zigzagged ahead, crouching, but mostly crawling, machine guns resting across their arms to ensure no sound.

Without warning, searchlights blasted skywards, the faint drone of aircraft engines drifted on the night air. Shriver had ducked instantly as the lights burst into life, his first thought, that they had been detected. He initially waited that split second when burning hot metal pierced his body – but no. His mind then realised it was an air raid – not now, not tonight!

Although he would do anything for the Fatherland he expected to die! His thoughts doubted the sense in bombing the docks tonight of all nights. "What more do those idiots want me to contend with," he spoke out loud to himself, in a whisper.

Salthouse and Albert Docks became alive with urgent activity, anti-aircraft gunners raised the triple A barrels to the sky. Each battery crew fixed on the dark sky, following the beam of the searchlights. As soon as they locked on, the gunners hoped the lights would retain the craft in their paths, giving them half a chance at recording a hit.

Suddenly one battery opened up, the silence broken, shells traced into the night.

The drone above was deafening now, together with the rat-tat-tat from the ground guns. Shriver saw his chance. Signalling his men, they broke cover and ran to the quay edge, dropping down in an instant, straight into a landing boat. Using their commando style daggers, the mooring ropes were cut. Shriver reached the pilot's position. "Stupid Englanders!" he said, "they even leave the key in place."

In a second he had started the engine, engaged a gear and, with his men safely aboard, the boat was pushed away from the quay and burst into life, spitting a jet of white water from the stern, mixing with a plume of black smoke as they met rising upwards. The boat sped from the quay, heading directly for the dock entrance.

Admiralty guards opened fire with small arms, revolvers and Enfield rifles. Corporal Sam Burton cranked the Vickers round and opened up. He wasn't firing in short bursts now, he was intent on emptying the whole belt of ammunition.

The whistle from the sky was unmistakable, the Luftwaffe had commenced unleashing their payloads. Coming inland from the River Mersey, the explosions started to rip through the dockland area, one after another, until the explosions were more or less indistinguishable, sounding like one continuous explosion.

The ground shook.

Albert Dock warehouses were ripped apart, gone in an instant, incendiary bombs turning bricks and mortar and iron and steel into molten lava, a red hot inferno. Some landed in the water inside the docks, water instantly turning to a foaming, volcanic-like pool, plumes of water rising a hundred foot in the air.

The noise intensified. The Prince of Wales, out in the Mersey, opened fire with her main guns, four foot flames leaping skywards from the gun barrels. Captain Leach had ordered the gunners to target the Luftwaffe.

Captain Siddlington-Brown was shouting orders. Sam Burton didn't flinch, he continued blasting away into the dock area. Only the fact that the Vickers was a water-cooled weapon prevented the barrel from illuminating with the heat.

As the air raid continued, fire engines' bells rang out, distant voices shouting and screaming, more and more explosions pounded the city, docks and surrounding areas.

A fierce battle raged at ground level too.

The fighting was continuing from the river.

Dingle station master Mr Potter had heard the battle from the docks. Freddie had still not been located. He knew in his own mind that he was at or near the docks. He had also taken young Grace there, too. *Not good!* he thought.

Running through the streets, jumping over fire hoses snaking across the roads, stumbling over bricks and stone, splashing through pools of water, fires raged, smoke filled the air. Fire crews rushing round, ambulance men tending the injured.

It was what it was – a war zone.

Finally, with the docks in sight, Mr Potter stopped to take a breath. His lungs filled with acrid smoke. Sweating and exhausted, he crouched over, leaning on his knees. He gulped as much air as possible. "I'm too old for all this!" he said.

The ground battle noise burst through the air. Clearly all hell was breaking loose on the dock as well as from the sky. The relentless rat-tat-tat from heavy machine guns, the zing from Enfield rifles and some small arms fire; it was hard to deduce who was firing at whom.

Slowly zinging along Salthouse Quay, Mr Potter spotted movement ahead. Through the fluctuating light he saw Freddie.

"My boy! Stay there, I'm coming!"

Startled by the shout, Freddie whipped round. Coming through the smoke and haze he saw Mr Potter, his face blackened from smoke, face dripping with sweat, clothes covered in dust.

"Mr Potter!"

Raising his hand and arm to his head and face, Potter acted as if he was avoiding incoming shots, but none were actually being aimed at him.

"Stay there, lad." Potter moved closer. "Where is Grace?"

"She's here with me."

Out from the shadows, the little girl appeared, dishevelled but safe.

"Thank goodness!" Mr Potter was relieved, to say the least. Both were safe – or as safe as could be in the battle zone.

Death from the sky still fell at an alarming rate. The air raid was still coming, wave after wave of Luftwaffe, unleash their deadly payloads. It looked like the city of Liverpool was being bombed into submission.

"Mr Potter – the Germans! They have taken a boat from the quay. They're trying to get out onto the river."

"So it seems, young fella."

"We have to stop them!"

"Now wait just a minute, Freddie."

"No, we have to stop them!" Freddie started to move away towards the dock gates. "We have to get the gates closed."

"Wait!" a voice boomed from the darkness. Sergeant Struthers appeared, tunic open and blood coming from a clear head wound. "Wait. Just where do you think you're going?"

"We have to stop the Germans!" Freddie shouted, showing a mixture of fear and excitement.

"Look around you, Freddie – we'll be lucky to survive this night, let alone stop the Germans." Struthers stumbled slightly, faint from his blood loss.

"Sergeant, you're hurt. Sit awhile," Mr Potter interrupted.

"No time, no time," Sergeant Struthers answered.

The landing boat engine roared with sheer power. Throttles on full, the boat sped towards the dock entrance gates. Oberleutnant Shriver shouted an order. One private moved to the bow of the boat and positioned a K98 rifle grenade launcher to his shoulder.

"Take out the dock gun!" he shouted.

"Yes, Oberleutnant," came the instant reply.

The Admiralty guards, manning the stone-built gun emplacement covering the dock entrance, trained the weapon on the speed boat. "Fire!"

In a flash .50 mm shells burst into the docks, strafing the British landing boat. Still it continued on, hurtling towards open water.

"Fire!" the German commander shouted.

The trigger clicked and a split second later the recoil rocked the soldier as the deadly grenade released. A smoke trail followed its path, en route to demolish the gun emplacement.

"Close the gates!" This was the last order from the emplacement guard, then silence.

The quayside gun lit the skyline as it exploded. The Admiralty guards did not, could not survive such a blow.

"Sergeant – look!" Freddie pointed towards the dock entrance. "We have to close the gates."

"The boy is right, Sergeant. If we don't, they're away," Mr Potter agreed with young Freddie.

"Right. Freddie, Potter, you two that side. I'll go to the left. Let's get these bloody gates locked up."

As they started to move off, "Oi – careful!" Struthers looked genuinely scared.

Potter just nodded.

The current air raid had raged now for close to ten minutes, the air thick with smoke. Red and orange flames filled the sky. Running at full pace, Freddie and Mr Potter covered the right-hand side of Salthouse Quay in record time. They had made the dock entrance.

On the other hand, Sergeant Struthers, feeling the effects of his head wound, was slower. He could see through the chaos that Potter and Freddie were already in place. Potter was frantically cranking the manual wheel. Inch by inch the gates to the right were closing. Watching Struthers' slow progress to the left, 'Come on man, come on!"

Finally, Sergeant Struthers reached the cranking wheel. Feeling weak now, he started to turn the wheel, after only two turns, he fell.

Shots rang out from the landing boat. Machine guns opened up, the Germans were not giving up quietly. The invading enemy splattered the quay side with rapid fire. They knew they had to keep the gates fully open, or at least one side.

Struthers had been hit – how hard? He fell like a stone.

The Germans were closer to escape.

"Good God!" Mr Potter shouted. He knew there was only one option; he or Freddie had to get to the other side. It was a hell of a leap!

"My boy, there is no way I can jump the gap between the gate and the side. I hate to ask…"

"Yes!" Freddie interrupted. With that he was already back tracking, giving himself a really good run at it.

"It's ten feet or so, lad. Do you think you can make it?"

Chapter Sixteen

HMS Prince of Wales was powering her turbines. Captain Leach had been ordered to break off his assault on the incoming aircraft, and cease his search for U-534.

His new orders were to steam at 'all ahead' towards Albert Dock to intercept the escaping Germans. She was still at general quarters, all guns manned. Lurching through the moderate swell, the Prince manoeuvred deeper along the Mersey, powering her way towards a city burning.

Intercept the German landing party at all costs. Capture or kill.

Captain Leach was aware now of the audacious Nazi plan from his recent orders and the fact his intelligence officers had gained information from the rescued submariners. He also learned that Kapitan Nollau had gone down with his boat. The prisoners confirmed this.

He was also fully aware that the German landing troops had nowhere to go!

In a strange way, he felt respect for the U-boat commander, eluding allied shipping, with stealth navigating the river and being able to launch inflatables at night, with no prior knowledge of the hazards that made up the tidal entrance to this great city. An experienced submariner, to say the least. But this was war! Whilst respecting him, he had had to destroy this invader – and that is exactly what he did to great effect.

The same thought process now applied to the Nazi landing party.

Her bow slicing through the water, the Prince surged on and on.

The drone overhead had faded. Clearly the Luftwaffe had done their night's work and were heading home. How many, if any, had been shot down, didn't concern Leach. The Royal Air Force had their part to play, his concern again was on the water.

A city in flames guided him towards the docks. "Comm, radio." The loudspeaker burst into life.

"Go ahead," he answered.

"Comm, radio. I have an eyes only message from the Admiralty."

"Roger that."

Captain Leach knew that an eyes only message was for the Captain only and a priority order from the top.

"You have the bridge, Number One."

"Aye, sir."

Making his way briskly but with an air of calm, Leach reached the radio room. The operator immediately rose to his feet and waited outside.

Captain Leach held the printout and studied the content; brief and to the point.

"CITY ON ITS KNEES, STOP. GERMAN INFILTRATORS ENGAGED, STOP. ESCAPE IMMINENT, STOP. MUCH COLLATERAL DAMAGE, STOP. IMPERATIVE YOU ELIMINATE, STOP. AT ALL COSTS, STOP."

Returning to the bridge, "All stop," Leach snapped out the order, still clutching the printout.

"All stop, aye."

The forward surging ceased and the engines fell quiet. The Prince slowed. Captain Leach snatched his binoculars and strode outside the bridge. Protocol dictated his executive officer accompanied him. The cool air took their breath away for a second.

The Port of Liverpool was burning. The heat travelled on the breeze. The sudden air chill was replaced with a warm feel and touch to the skin. The heat from the burning fuel and all manner of combustibles stored in the warehouses fuelled the

German incendiaries. The city would be burning for many hours to come.

Leach showed the printout to his number one. "Thoughts?" he said.

"Numerous, sir!"

"Care to share them?"

"Permission to speak freely, sir?"

"Go ahead, Number One. It's just me and you."

"What the hell do they want us to do? Blast them out of the water? Smacks of murder to me, sir!"

"My thoughts exactly," Leach responded.

"Isn't that against the Geneva Convention?" He paused, then, "That makes us no better than Jerry, sir."

"Permission to speak freely is now withdrawn, Number One." Leach snatched the printout back. "That'll be all, Number One."

Chapter Seventeen

Freddie had started his run. He could see the stolen landing boat hurtling towards the single open river gate. Mr Potter willed the young lad to make the leap. Ten feet was ten feet, he was convinced it was too far for Freddie to make. But he willed him to succeed anyway.

Freddie reached the closed gate, running hard across the top. His last step was the start of his leap. Into the air he rose, summoning all his strength to succeed. Letting out a shout, he reached the other side. Luckily the gate was two feet thick, which shortened the distance by two feet. Freddie hit the gate, his hands smashing into the wooden top and gripping tightly.

To fall was not an option.

His feet dangled four feet above the cold water and the landing boat was still smashing through the water, heading for escape. He glanced to his left and saw a German putting a gun to his shoulder and taking aim. If he didn't move, he was surely dead!

The Germans were fifty feet from the gates now and so much closer to being successful in their escape.

Freddie started hauling himself up, then, "Gotcha." A broad hand grabbed his right wrist. Home Guard Private Billy Turpin spoke confidently. "Come on, son, give me your other hand."

Freddie looked up straight into the eyes of this familiar face and gave a smile.

"Quickly now!" Turpin said.

The tired boy was hauled onto the quay as if he weighed no more than a small piece of balsa wood.

"Where did you come from?" Freddie asked.

"Later," replied Turpin. "Grab the wheel. Let's get this lump of wood shut."

"Yes, sir." Freddie did what he was told and both he and the private started to crank the iron wheel round and round. Slowly the left-hand dock gate started to move, pushing the water back inside the dock.

The Germans were now just twenty feet from freedom.

A shot rang out. The German trooper had unleashed the K98 rifle grenade.

The violent heaving of the landing boat made aiming a weapon hit and miss. The explosive grenade had missed, disappearing through the gap in the dock gates, and flying aimlessly out into the river.

Before he could reload, Oberleutnant Shriver had veered the boat hard to the right. Wash slammed into the dock walls, sending spray into the air.

The gates were now fully closed. The small group of Nazi invaders was trapped. They had nowhere to go.

Chapter Eighteen

Captain Leach raced back inside the bridge. "Incoming contact, sir!" The voice over the radio was hurried.

"What the hell?" Leach was caught off guard. "Where and what?" he shouted into the handset.

"Sonar contact astern, one thousand yards and closing." After a second, "Fish in the water, sir!"

"Hard-a-port!' he yelled. "Chief, get the damned power up. Full, now!"

"Sonar, Comm; seven five zero yards and closing fast. Second contact one hundred yards, bearing 243. Confirm two torpedoes in the water."

"Chief, I need full power now! Helm, right full rudder!"

"Aye."

"Right full rudder, aye sir."

The Prince of Wales' turn was so tight the crew hung onto anything they could to prevent being side slipped from their stations. Thick black smoke billowed up as she came under full power; the turbines raged.

"Sonar, Comm; two five zero yards and closing."

"Chief, red line it or we're dead in the water!" Leach slammed the handset down.

"Sonar, Comm; five zero yards bearing 243."

"Twenty yards!"

"Sound collision!" Captain Leach ordered. "Brace for impact. Brace, brace, brace!"

The collision alert klaxon announced imminent contact.

"Sonar, Comm; ten yards, five – three – one…" The sonar operator fell silent. "Missed!"

Leach and his number one glanced at each other, sweating and clearly nervous. Leach shouted, "Hard left rudder – come about, full ahead."

"Sonar, Comm: second contact four hundred yards, bearing 243."

The Prince straightened for a few seconds and then, under full power, sent her crew sliding to the left and she banked hard, smashed her way through her own wake.

"Sonar, one five zero yards bearing 243."

Ping after ping, the sonar equipment went into overdrive, louder and louder as the second torpedo raced beneath the waves towards the Prince.

"Seventy-five yards – closing!"

"Roger," Leach answered, although no answer was necessary.

"Thirty yards."

"All hands, brace for impact." Number One spoke into the ship-wide intercom.

"Ten, nine, eight, seven, six, five, four, three, two, one…"

"Are we hit?" Number One shouted.

There was no explosion, just a loud thud. No fireball, no listing, nothing.

"A dud!" The executive officer rushed outside the bridge, binoculars to his face. "It was a dud, Captain, it bounced off us, bearing 254."

"What's the arming ranging on those fish?" Leach asked.

"One thousand yards, sir."

"He was too close, he got it wrong!" Leach knew the submariner commander had miscalculated, or he had just snapped off two shots.

"He was too damn close," Leach repeated. "Helm, come to starboard ten. Ramming speed."

"Aye aye, sir."

As the Prince came round, her elegant bow parted the water like a knife through butter, steaming seaward. Leach and his number one were viewing the waters ahead.

"There, Skipper. Four hundred yards dead ahead!" His number one pointed ahead.

Grasping the intercom, Captain Leach spoke calmly. "All hands brace for collision. Helm, maintain present course. Chief, more speed, give her everything."

"Aye, but we are at one hundred and ten percent now, sir."

"Blow the damn turbines if you have to, red line it, Chief." Leach was determined that this clever U-Boat kapitan would not fool him a second time.

"Sonar, Comm: she's turning, Captain. Ten degrees port."

"Helm, adjust course."

"Sir. Adjusting, ten degrees port, aye."

"One two five yards."

"Nine five yards."

"Thirty yards."

"All hands; collision," Leach shouted.

Even though bracing, the bridge crew were flung across the floor upon impact. Electromagnetic pulses splashed through equipment, arcing electrical flashes shot across the bridge, screens exploded, the bridge windows shattered, air and sea spray flashed inside, causing more short circuits.

The Prince of Wales slammed into the starboard side of the U-boat just ahead of the stern, cutting through her like a diamond-tipped drill. The U-boat rolled violently; her back was broken. Her bow rose from the water some twenty feet, as if the whole boat had been dragged from the water by the force of the collision.

The Prince continued, full power thrashing through metal. The sounds of grating metal on metal proved unbearable for the sonar operator. He yanked his headphones from his ears.

The water around the collision site erupted. Explosions melted some of the side-board railings on the foredeck. The Prince couldn't stop now even if she wanted to. She ploughed straight through the submarine.

More and more explosions as fuel ignited and stored torpedoes burst through the U-boat outer skin, ripping the boat apart. The river was on fire. More explosions, more flames splurging into the night sky, super-heated water washing the ship's deck. Then it was gone!

"All stop!" commanded Leach.

"Lookouts to the bridge," the bridge officer ordered.

U-534, or what was left of her, sank from view. The River Mersey extinguished her flames, heating the surrounding water, which boiled like a cauldron.

This was not a fake. U534 was no more!

An eerie silence descended. The bridge crew were silent.

"Come about, Number One. Look for survivors." Captain Leach spoke softly. Deep down he felt some sympathy for this adversary. This was a brave and talented kapitan, and brave men had perished this day. Davy Jones' locker came to mind.

This enemy submariner had shown courage and tactical awareness. He had lured Captain Leach into a false sense of security, and very nearly given his fellow Germans something to shout about. The propaganda which could have been achieved with the sinking of a British Navy destroyer in English waters would have been invaluable to the German war machine.

However, that was not to be.

"Score one for the good guys, Captain."

"Yes! Thank you, Number One. Any signs of survivors?"

"Negative, sir," one lookout responded.

Positioned some one hundred metres from the Albert Dock entrance, HMS Prince of Wales came to all stop.

"Dock gates appear secured, sir," lookout number two announced.

"Roger that," Leach replied.

"Ready starboard .50 cals," number one ordered.

One by one the eight starboard .50 calibre crews confirmed their readiness.

"If anything comes out of those gates blast it to high hell!" Captain Leach directed the eight crews. He had no idea what was happening on the other side of the gates. He would not get caught with his pants down again.

Peering through the shattered bridge windows, Leach and his number one watched intently, whilst listening to damage control messages on the intercom. Sections were reporting in one by one. The port side screws had sustained damage and were non-operational, engine room sailors had closed off the turbines; clearly the Prince was going nowhere very quickly.

Most electrical systems on the bridge had burnt out, sonar was non-operational, main weapons control was gone. The deck guns were manual and could still be operational. More reports came in for non-working equipment.

"When this day is over, Number One, I suspect we'll be getting some shore leave!" Captain Leach offered.

"Roger that, sir. Going to be dry docked for a while."

Chapter Nineteen

The German landing party circled inside the dock, trapped like a caged animal, the on-board crew firing wildly in all directions.

Captain Siddlington-Brown was now in control, the dock was sealed, the Home Guard and Admiralty guards in position. There was no need for return fire. "Platoon, cease fire. Cease fire!"

Major Plaistow arrived with his regular soldiers. His men marched two prisoners, Sergeant Franz Schmidt supporting a wounded private. They had supplied a courageous rear guard action for the Fatherland; however in the face of overwhelming odds they had decided surrender was preferable to death. Following their actions, there would be no disgrace.

"This is how the real soldiers do it, Siddlington-Brown!" Plaistow boasted.

"And this is how the Home Guard volunteers do it, sir!" came the reply, as he pointed to the enclosed dock. "Better keep your head down, sir. They are not quite ready to be reeled in yet."

Firing from the landing boat eased. Their limited ammunition failing, still they continued circling the inner dock.

"Burton, have you got them in your sights?" Captain Siddlington-Brown questioned.

"I have, sir," came his reply.

"Keep it that way."

Will do, Captain." Burton cocked the Vickers again.

Striding erect and with an air of confidence, Siddlington-Brown came out from his place of cover and stood at the edge of the quay. Occupants of the landing boat watched.

Oberleutnant Shriver throttled down the craft's engine. With a hand gesture, his crew lowered their weapons. Dawn was breaking. An eerie silence fell upon this unlikely change of circumstances.

"Sir!" Captain Siddlington-Brown directed his word towards the water and the German officer. "Sir, it's over! You are confined to this dock, low on ammunition and, finally, your means of escape has been destroyed." As if to emphasise the point he continued, "U-534 has been rammed and sunk by the Royal Navy. You cannot escape our island."

He waited for a response.

The Oberleutnant spoke in German to his men. Calmly and controlled, without question, each of his men aboard the landing boat placed their weapon on the deck and stepped back.

"Herr Captain, it is, how do you say, game set and match, I believe."

"Yes, sir, I do believe that to be the case." His words were spoken to a formal salute. Shriver reciprocated the gesture.

"Kindly bring the craft to the quay."

The seized landing boat was steered gently to the dock wall and ropes were thrown aloft, gratefully caught by the Home Guard Volunteer Force. The boat was tied off and secured.

British weapons all pointed in one direction; the figures standing aboard the small craft.

Major Plaistow stepped forward, hoping to now take control. This would be a very large feather in his cap, the capture of infiltrating saboteurs. "Place your hands on your heads," he ordered.

Captain Siddlington-Brown was dumbfounded. This pompous little man was trying to take all the praise. Then something strange happened.

"With respect, Major, I will only offer my surrender to that man and his platoon," pointing to Siddlington-Brown, followed by a sweeping arm motion towards the Home Guard troops on the quayside.

Seizing the moment, "Oberleutnant, if you please, one at a time, please instruct your men to climb the ladder," Siddlington-Brown gently but firmly gave his instruction.

As each Nazi soldier climbed the quay ladder and stood proud on the stone quayside, Siddlington-Brown ordered one of his men to take them into custody, securing their hands behind their backs. All the time the Vickers was trained on the boat.

When all Germans were out of the boat, Private Billy Turpin was ordered down to collect their weapons.

Standing face to face, Oberleutnant Shriver straightened his clothing, then stood to attention and saluted. "Sir, my men and I are now your prisoners of war."

"Thank you," came the reply.

Major Plaistow had been side-lined and he didn't much like it, but despite his protests, he clearly wasn't going to receive any credit for this result. Red-faced and feeling completely surplus to requirements, he took several steps to the rear.

Freddie Bloom was kneeling over his friend, Sergeant Struthers, lying motionless on the quay. He was face down in a pool of blood. With the gates closed and secured, Mr Potter ran across and tried to pull Freddie away. "Don't look, my lad."

"Medic, we need a medic here now!" Mr Potter shouted back towards Siddlington-Brown.

Admiralty guards took control of the prisoners and Sam Burton left the Vickers and ran over to his sergeant. Billy Turpin was already there and trying to revive his fallen friend.

He knew from the blood loss; there was no hope for his pal. "Sarge! Come on, Sarge!"

Nothing.

Captain Siddlington-Brown made his excuses to his German prisoner and doubled timed across the quay. In the course of events he had failed to notice his trusted sergeant had been shot. As he neared the motionless body, his heart sank. This was personal now! A comrade in arms fallen.

"He's gone, Sam, there's nothing you can do." Mr Potter was quietly spoken.

"Medic, where's the bloody medic?" Turpin screamed, pushing his hand still harder over the open bullet wounds in his chest.

"Captain, for God's sake, get the medic!" Turpin pleaded.

"Easy, lad. A medic will do him no good now." Siddlington-Brown tried to avoid being matter of fact, but that's how the words came out.

"No! There was no need for him to die! Why? Why did he have to die?"

Placing a reassuring hand on his shoulder, Captain Siddlington-Brown was clearly shaken, whether that was from the heat of battle, or just plain sadness that a member of his platoon had died doing his duty. The Captain was a proud man, proud of his men, proud of his country and proud of a young civilian boy who had shown exceptional bravery in the face of danger, during an air raid too. Last night had been a good night for British morale and further resolution that victory would be theirs.

However, an overwhelming feeling of remorse and sadness filled his head and heart at the death of a good man, who had only a few short hours earlier been ordering the platoon and directing their repair efforts at Dingle railway station.

As Sam Burton walked away, head bowed, looking like a tired and beaten man, he heard, "We will honour him, Private. We will not forget." Siddlington-Brown snapped to attention at the side of the limp figure and held a salute.

Private Billy Turpin eased his friend to the ground, then stood erect and held a salute for well over a minute.

Mr Potter coaxed Freddie away and slowly walked him along the quay. "Come lad, your mother will be worried."

Major Plaistow approached Siddlington-Brown. Without a word, he too snapped out and held a salute. After a moment he said, "To the fallen."

The German prisoners were marched to waiting trucks. They would be interrogated and later imprisoned for the duration of the war. For them, they would live through it. Others were not so lucky.

Then the unexpected; with the gathered prisoners and armed guards grouped closely together, Oberleutnant Wilhelm Shriver grappled for a sidearm of a guard – a soldier of the Admiralty guard no less – and drew the weapon from its holster. Raising the weapon, he stepped to the side and pointed the revolver in the direction of the British officers.

"Herr Captain!" Shriver spoke in a raised voice.

Both Siddlington-Brown and Major Plaistow looked across the quayside. Sam Burton stopped in his tracks. Private Turpin reacted first. This was exactly what Shriver wanted!

Turpin's anger exploded. He raced towards the Vickers gun still on the quay. In an instant he spun it round and let loose with a short sharp burst of fire!

Shriver went down, the revolver sprang from his grasp, the prisoners and their guards dived for cover. The next instant voices shouted.

"Stand down, Private!" Siddlington-Brown ordered. "Secure that weapon."

For what seemed an age, no-one moved; then the inactivity was broken as the guards ordered the prisoners away. Major Plaistow looked shell shocked. Sam Burton stood starring at Turpin, who just seemed to be gazing into a void, an empty, faraway look in his eyes.

"Easy, Billy!" Burton moved slowly towards his colleague. "Easy mate, take it easy."

Private Turpin never moved.

"Private, stand to." Captain Siddlington-Brown spoke calmly and quietly.

"Burton, stay with him," he said in a more assertive tone.

"Sir," came the reply.

Captain Siddlington-Brown moved swiftly towards his prisoner. Seeing slight movement, he bent down and spoke to his German captive. "Easy Oberleutnant, a medic's coming." He shouted, "Medic, medic!"

Hobnail boots resounded off the cobbled quay. An army corps medic appeared. Kneeling beside the German, he thrust wadding into the gunshot wounds, trying to stem the blood flow; he clearly knew it was of no use!

"Herr Captain, please…" Shriver gestured for Siddlington-Brown to come closer. "Captain, I could not surrender. My orders were to fight to the death. I could not let my men be sacrificed on the whim of a madman, therefore I failed. I could not ever return home in disgrace…" He paused.

"Don't talk," the Captain offered.

The medic looked at his officer and then lowered his eyes. The German wasn't going to make it.

"Captain, please treat my men under the Geneva Convention. They were acting under my orders. This is war, not personal." Shriver ceased talking and fell silent.

"He's gone, sir." The medic stated the obvious.

"Damn!" Siddlington-Brown rose to his feet.

The Admiralty guard re-secured the dock. Information was already being received regarding the sinking of U-534 and the heroism of the Royal Navy.

There were heroes elsewhere this day.

"Captain, please walk with me." The major held out a friendly arm. "If you please, Captain."

Siddlington-Brown quietly, if reluctantly, obeyed and moved away from the body at his feet.

"The ambulance crew will tend to your sergeant now," the major said.

"There will be a full debrief. London will want to know exactly what happened here over the last two days or so. How they managed to land? How the Nazis were able to get a submarine so close to our shores? Security at the docks? Each of your men will be interviewed, as will mine. You and I will be put under severe scrutiny. I need to know what exactly you, as Home Guard commanding officer, will say?" Talking as they walked, Plaistow seemed very nervous.

"Major, with all due respect! This is not the time or the place!"

"Captain! As your senior officer…"

"Go to hell, sir!" Captain Siddlington-Brown interrupted his major in a less than respectful manner.

The captain returned to the lifeless body of his sergeant.

Mr Potter had removed his railway tunic and placed it gently over the body of Sergeant Struthers, firstly to hide the vision from young Freddie Bloom, secondly, as a mark of respect and affording him some dignity in death.

"Come on, son, I'll take to your mum. She will be waiting for you."

"Why, Mr Potter?" Freddie spoke through a cracking voice, tear-filled eyes pleading with Mr Potter.

"I know, lad. It's all so bloody pointless. The sooner we defeat this madman, the sooner this damn war will be over." The madman referred to was, of course, Adolf Hitler. "He is a very dangerous man who, through indoctrination, has convinced the German people they are superior. People without Germanic features and ancestry are treated like something their jackboots have trodden in."

Freddie looked a little confused.

"What I mean, laddie, is he believes if you are not German, you have no right to live and breathe. He is a mad murderer with no remorse and no respect for life." After a short pause he went on, "Sergeant Struthers believed this and gave the ultimate sacrifice. He was a very brave man. Take comfort in that, Freddie."

With one last look back at his friend, Freddie dried his eyes. His thoughts dragged back on hearing a familiar voice.

"Freddie! Freddie."

"Grace, you're okay?" The first time for a while, Freddie was able to smile; he had forgotten about her when he had raced away with Mr Potter heading for the river gates.

Looking up, Mr Potter produced a beaming smile; he was relieved she was safe. "Go on lad, I'll catch you up."

"Grace, Grace, did you see what happened?" Freddie ran along the quayside.

"No, I had my eyes closed the whole time." Grace was so excited to see him again. Jumping up and down on the spot she couldn't contain her joy. When Freddie reached her, he was relieved, excited, sad and happy, all at the same time.

"I helped to save the docks."

"What? How? What did you do?" Grace didn't really understand what had happened. All she knew was that bad men had come, bombs were falling and soldiers were firing guns.

"I got the gates closed. I jumped across the dock, I was dodging bullets and bombs! The Germans were in the boat, there was a warship on the river! Didn't you see any of it?"

"Are you making this all up?"

"Course not, how could I make it up?"

Mr Potter caught up to them, just catching the last part of their conversation. "It's all true, Grace. Young Freddie here is a hero. He saved us, he deserves a medal!"

"Cor! Do you think I'll get one, Mr Potter?"

"I should expect so," Potter said, with a wry grin on his face. "I should expect so."

Freddie fell silent for a moment, as he watched his friend being carried away on a stretcher towards a black painted ambulance. A caring hand touched his shoulder.

"Come on, you two, your mothers will be waiting, and I really need a cup of tea."

"And biscuits?" Grace added.

"We'll see what Mrs Potter can rummage up."

Walking from the docks, they saw Sam Burton with his arm around Billy Turpin, still standing next to the Vickers. Lives had been changed here this day, forever.

Mr Potter, Freddie and Grace paused briefly, giving them a forced smile.

Having dismissed himself from the presence of Major Plaistow, Captain Siddlington-Brown hurried towards Freddie, Grace and Mr Potter and immediately snapped to attention and held a formal salute for one full moment.

"Freddie, please accept my grateful thanks for your actions this night. I would like to take this opportunity to make you an unofficial private in the Home Guard Volunteer Force."

The biggest smile ever beamed across Freddie Bloom's face. Coming to attention, he mimicked a salute and said, "Thank you, sir."

Captain Siddlington-Brown performed a smart about turn and marched off, re-joining Major Plaistow.

Chapter Twenty

Mrs Janet Bloom didn't know whether to smack or hug Freddie when Mr Potter returned him and Grace to Dingle railway station.

"Thank God you're safe, both of you. Where have you been? What have you been up to?"

"There there, missus, let the boy catch his breath. He's had a busy old night, with saving the world and all that!" Potter winked at Mrs Bloom.

"Sorry Mum, but as a member of the Home Guard, I had to follow the action…"

"You're not in the Home Guard."

Freddie interrupted her. "Oh yes I am. Ask Captain Siddlington-Brown."

"What are you going on about?"

"I believe the captain has commissioned young Freddie here, following his courageous action at the docks last night. I think there may be a medal in it for him!" Mr Potter interrupted the conversation.

"What!" Mrs Bloom shouted. "Medal? What medal?"

"He is a hero. Freddie saved the day and countless lives, I hasten to add."

"Mr Potter, what on earth are you talking about?" Mrs Bloom questioned.

Always knowing the perfect moment, Mrs Potter came onto the platform carrying a tray with lemonade, cups and glasses, and a nice pot of hot tea.

"There we are then, who wants a nice drink?"

"Perfect, Mrs Potter. Lovely, just what we need," said Mr Potter.

Not one to publicly show her feelings, Mrs Potter was so relieved her husband had returned safe and well, she gave him a kiss on the cheek.

"Steady on, old girl!" Mr Potter said.

A strange quiet filled the air, the sun breaking through – no bells, no bombs, no gun shots and no running round. It all felt a little surreal to Freddie, to be sat on the station platform with family and friends drinking lemonade.

"Well, will you look at you two!" Mrs Potter placed her hands on her hips and sighed.

Feeling as though she was letting the side down, Mrs Bloom produced her hanky and gave a little spit to it then, as mothers did, started wiping her son's face. She was and always would be a proud lady who believed in cleanliness.

"Mum!" Freddie protested.

"Go with it, lad." Mr Potter smiled and winked at him. "Your mum has been worried," he whispered.

Freddie gave a nod in understanding. He then threw both arms around his Mum's waist and gave her a massive hug. "Love you, Mum."

The station telephone rang out and broke the silence. Mr Potter hurried to the ticket office and answered it. Mrs Potter, Mrs Bloom, Mrs Bagworth, Freddie and Grace all looked on, hearing only the muted voice of the station master.

It was one of those strange incidents; after the intense bombing the night before, the telephone lines were still working. Sometimes things like that happen, everything around can be obliterated, yet one single item or building escapes untouched. Clearly the telephone lines fell into this category.

Less than a minute later, Mr Potter reappeared on the platform, pausing briefly. He had a rather grim look on his dusty and blackened face; Mrs Potter had yet to take her hanky and spit to his dirty face. He looked long and hard at the seated group.

"Well, there you are!" he spoke quietly.

"Oh my! What is it, Mr Potter?" His wife had fear in her voice.

The gathered group felt an air of trepidation; bad news? What could be worse than what they had been through last night? No-one spoke, but all eyes were fixed on the station master. They watched and waited, fearful to ask, afraid of what the answer may be.

Walking with a tired gait, Mr Potter edged closer to the group, watching his feet. Not daring to look directly at them, Mr Potter mopped his brow and ran his fingers through his silvering hair.

"Oh, my word! Mr Potter, you certainly don't look like the cat that got the cream!" his wife offered. "What on earth has happened?" she questioned.

"Not good, my dear, seems like one of the Nazis has escaped. He overpowered the guards, killed two of them, and disappeared."

"After all we went through," Freddie shouted.

"Shoosh!" whispered his mother. "Let Mr Potter finish."

"That was the guard house on the phone. Information has been passed to the military and police. They wanted to let us know and told me not to worry." He paused, then went on, "They are confident they will recapture him very soon."

The relaxed mood soon changed. The seated group suddenly exuded an air of hopelessness.

Mr Potter finally reached the table, looked at the fear contained in every single eye of the gathered group, and more so in the emptiness seen inside Freddie Bloom. Mr Potter realised he had taken the prank too far. His performance had clearly been masterful – believable!

"Oh dear! Seems I miscalculated the mood here! Friends, it's all right! Honestly, it's all right, I was joking. There has been no escape, no killings and certainly no need to worry. The Germans are safely in custody. They are being interviewed by Military Intelligence. The Admiralty wanted to congratulate young Freddie here, and request that he and the rest of us attend the Admiralty Offices in Lord Street tomorrow. I believe the Home Guard has received the same request."

"You!" Mrs Potter was clearly annoyed.

"Mr Potter you gave me a heart attack then, I hope you realise that?" Mrs Bloom said, as she wiped a tear from her cheek.

"I'm sorry all!" An air of guilt filled the station master.

"Nice one, Mr Potter, you had us going then." Freddie gave a hearty belly laugh.

"Glad you still have the famous scouse humour, my lad."

A little red-faced, Mr Potter took his seat at the table and stretched. It had been a very long night and day. He was now feeling exhausted.

In the days which followed, although the air raids continued, preparations were made in the highest security conditions, for a visit by War Office staff to Liverpool.

Among the VIPs attending the city was the First Lord of the Admiralty and Prime Minister, Winston Churchill. He was to be accompanied by high ranking military officials and local government officials. News of the events had very quickly reached the halls of Westminster.

Mr Churchill had long been keen to promote acts of bravery and courage by groups and individuals. This was a morale booster for the British people in general. It showed that the nation was not and would not surrender to Nazi aggression.

The pounding Britain had taken and indeed was still taking was creating great pain and suffering for the general public. Food shortages, bombed out homes and factories; people in general were not aware just how close the country was to defeat. Things not going well in the actual fighting, the German machine seemingly growing in strength.

Strength was gained through seeing how, in France, although under occupation, the resistance fighters continued in their attempts to disrupt the Nazi plan. The British knew our shores would be next and that could not be allowed to happen.

Mr Churchill arrived in Liverpool under heavy security and he met with the Bloom and Bagworth families in a private meeting, prior to the very public ceremony at the town hall. The Toxteth Volunteer Force were also to be honoured for their actions.

It was intended to be a 'tea and medals' moment, a very public boost for the war effort.

Mr Churchill also visited Dingle railway station and the docks. Local officials scurried round, eager to actually speak with the Prime Minister; all keen to overstate Liverpool's importance to the country's survival. Being graceful, Mr Churchill listened. His main objective was to publicly thank the Home Guard, Mr Potter, Grace Bagworth and of course Freddie Bloom, who had shown exceptional courage for a young boy in the face of this mighty foe.

After seeing the devastation first hand, he returned to the town hall and the ceremony got underway. He spoke for twenty minutes before he presented medals. The last medal was saved for the best. "Can Master Freddie Bloom please come to the platform," an official announced.

Shy but very proud, Freddie stepped up and walked to the steps. One by one he rose and stepped out onto the raised platform. The imposing figure of the Prime Minister stood before him – customary cigar gripped between his teeth.

"Now then young man, your actions, together with actions of the others before you, have shown the highest level of courage and bravery, a rare trait in one so young. Your actions cannot in any way be underestimated. Faced with great personal danger, the armed enemy on our shores, during a very intense air raid, you have shown little regard for your own safety but have acted for the greater good. For that, this country owes you a great debt of gratitude. It gives me the greatest pleasure to award you this small token of a nation's gratitude – and my personal gratitude – as we all say 'thank you Freddie Bloom'." Mr Churchill completed his speech with an outstretched hand which, after some prompting from his mum, Freddie took and smiled.

Captain Siddlington-Brown was the first to rise to his feet, applauding this very brave young man. The Home Guard stood as a unit. Mr Potter seemed to be clapping the loudest, the council dignitaries applauded more sedately. It now seemed that the whole audience was on its feet.

This was another day Freddie Bloom would never forget.

Epilogue

This story depicts but a small part of a world war which lasted for six years, with many millions of deaths – military and civilian alike. The true horrors of armed conflict only really come to light with the cessation of the fighting, with stories told by returning prisoners of war and survivors from the German prison camps.

According to historians the 1939-1945 war should never have happened. This was what the world had been told following the so called Great War 1914-1918, the war to end all wars.

But the Second World War did happen. People with larger egos, dreams of the 'superior race' and world domination; aggression fuelled by misguided beliefs, or religion or just plain madmen. It was the job of the free world to stand up and be counted and in so doing the cost was unimaginable, in financial terms, but more importantly, in human lives.

Freddie Bloom's story was not unique, of course, and what he was to see in the imminent future shaped the character of men throughout the free world. Accounts of heroism, determination, belief in what was right, and the plain need to survive, served to fuel the will and spirit of those at home, fighting a war in their own way.